BABY SURPRISE
FOR THE SPANISH
BILLIONAIRE

BABY SURPRISE FOR THE SPANISH BILLIONAIRE

JESSICA GILMORE

MILLS & BOON

First published in Great Britain 2018
by Mills & Boon, an imprint of HarperCollins*Publishers*
1 London Bridge Street, London, SE1 9GF

Large Print edition 2018

ISBN: 978-0-263-07393-5

MIX
Paper from
responsible sources
FSC® C007454

This book is produced from independently certified
FSC™ paper to ensure responsible forest management.
For more information visit www.harpercollins.co.uk/green.

Printed and bound in Great Britain
by CPI Group (UK) Ltd, Croydon, CR0 4YY

For Katy!

That was fun! Let's do it again some time…

CHAPTER ONE

ANNA GRAY CLASPED her coffee cup in both hands, stepped gingerly out onto the creaking veranda and stared around in dismay. The island resort had looked charmingly ramshackle in the purple of twilight when she'd first arrived last night, but daylight revealed a very different picture. The low, white bungalows dotted around, each in its own private grove, should have made a beautiful scene, but even the mellow sun of an early May morning couldn't paint La Isla Marina in flattering colours.

From her vantage point Anna could see all around right to the very tip of the island. The administrative buildings, including her mother's living quarters, were here at the palatial villa that marked the island's centre point, the swimming pools, tennis courts and relaxation areas all interspersed amongst the bungalows. If she stood on her tiptoes, Anna could just see the deep blue of the sea and the friendly waving of the palms that marked the beach boundaries. It was all so very nearly idyllic.

Very nearly… Until she looked a little closer and saw the reality behind the charm; the paint peeling off the whitewashed bungalows, the green shutters battered and hanging at odd angles. La Isla Marina was known for its lush greenery and profusion of flowers, but right now it resembled a jungle, not an upmarket resort. What had happened? True, everything had been a little faded when she was last here for her *abuelo's* funeral three years ago, but the hotel had still been recognisable as the idyllic magical place where she had run free every childhood summer.

The old familiar guilt prickled through her. She knew how disorganised her mother was, she should have foreseen this, not needed a tearful phone call begging her to come and help out.

The guilt intensified. It wasn't the unusual panic in her mother's voice that had persuaded her, it was Anna's own need for an escape, for time to think. If she hadn't been nearing crisis point would she have stayed in Oxford and allowed her mother to struggle on alone? She knew the answer to that. Every time they spoke her mother asked when she'd have time to come and visit, and Anna always found an excuse to put her off. Visiting La Isla Marina knowing neither grandparent would be there to greet her had been too hard to contemplate—and it wasn't as if she and Sancia were close. Nor, she knew, did Sancia have any intention of making an effort to come and visit Anna.

No, she'd responded to her mother's pleas for her own selfish reasons, thinking a few weeks of relaxing in the sun, away from the pressures of Oxford, were just what she needed. Her heart sank as she looked around at the wild and untamed bushes. Relaxing was the last thing she was going to be able to do.

'Good morning, *querida*, how did you sleep?'

Anna turned at the sound of her mother's voice. 'Great, thanks. I was tired after my journey.' She eyed her mother critically, noting the extra grey threading through Sancia Garcia's thick dark mane, the lines around her mother's eyes, lines which hadn't been there three years before. 'How are you?'

'Everything is wonderful.' Anna stiffened as her mother flung her arms around her, pulling her in close. 'I'm glad you're here, *querida*. It's been too long.'

'Yes, well…' Stepping back, Anna attempted to extract both herself and her miraculously un-spilt coffee. 'I've been busy, you know. With the book and teaching… What's happened, Mama?'

'Happened?'

Anna bit down on her irritation as her mother looked vaguely around the resort. This was how Sancia Garcia operated, floating through the world in a time and space of her own. She'd never seen why her daughters needed to be at school on time, or even why they needed to *attend* school if the sun was shining, why dinner should be planned and at a set time, the point of timetables. Anna hadn't yet turned ten when she realised that if they were to be like other families she needed to take charge, to be responsible for both herself and her sister, Rosa. Her chest tightened. Nothing had changed; she was a fool to hope it ever would.

Sancia had even managed to separate from

her husband in such a slow, dreamy way it almost seemed unintentional. And she never panicked, which was why her call for help was so out of character. Why Anna had booked the next flight over, leaving her father, her responsibilities, her teaching behind in Oxford. Not that Sancia seemed even slightly stressed now. Anna's grip tightened even more, the heat from the cup almost scalding her; no doubt as soon as Anna had shown up Sancia had thankfully abdicated all responsibility to her once again. 'To the hotel, Mama. It doesn't look like there's been any upkeep at all for goodness knows how long. How did it get to this stage?'

Sancia shrugged. 'You know Pedro retired when your *abuelo* died, then Bonita retired also and they both ran this place like clockwork. It's been hard to get staff to replace them, people who care, who stay. And everything happens at once, *querida*, one light breaks then another, then a toilet then the swimming pool filters and I just can't keep on top of it all.'

'No wonder bookings are down.' The real wonder was that anyone had booked to stay here at all. 'Why didn't you ask for help before?'

'You're so busy, you have your own life, Anna, as does your sister. I didn't want to worry you. I knew something would turn up and it has. This wedding will fix everything.' Her mother clasped her hands. 'The money, the publicity! The glamour! We can restore La Isla Marina to the way it was when I was young, when your grandparents first built the resort.'

The wedding. The magical ingredient on which her mother was banking all her hopes. The wedding she had agreed to host in exactly one month's time despite the island not being anywhere near ready. It would be bad enough, Anna thought, if this were any normal wedding. Only her mother would blithely take on the exclusive wedding of a supermodel and her millionaire fiancé. These people looked down on five-star luxury, and right now the island would barely scrape two stars.

'We have a lot of work to do before then. No one is going to want to have their dream wedding here, especially not some Internet sensation who posts every detail of their life online.' Anna looked behind her, peering through the half-opened door that led into the office. A career spent researching in libraries, a life of compiling footnotes and organising sources meant Anna had some pretty kickass admin skills. Her mother most likely needed budgets, accounting, marketing and day-to-day working rotas as soon as possible and Anna was just the girl to sort that out for her.

Of course there was the little question of fifty-two bungalows needing a lick of paint, a damn good clean and some DIY. Hopefully there was no need for Anna to get her hands dirty; DIY was not her forte. Luckily her sister was handy with a toolkit. 'When is Rosa getting here?' Anna's stomach clenched apprehensively as she waited for her mother to reply. She hadn't seen her sister in several years either, only in her case there weren't any weekly phone calls, not even the odd tag on social media. If Sancia had mentioned earlier that she had also begged Rosa to come and help, would Anna have agreed to come too? The truth was she had no idea. Three years was a long time, but she hadn't forgotten a single one of the bitter words she and her sister had exchanged back then. She wasn't eager for a repeat performance.

'As soon as she can. She's on an important assignment, you know. She said she wouldn't be able to get here in the next two weeks but she'll do her best to get here as soon as possible after that.'

Anna compressed her lips. Of course, whatever Rosa chose to do was important as far as their mother was concerned. She was always far more impressed by Rosa's unconventional approach to life than by Anna's achievements and qualifications. At twenty-eight she should be too old to be hurt by her mother's lack of interest in all Anna had worked so hard for. But Anna hadn't been able to help noticing that her mother's apartment was filled with framed copies of Rosa's photos—and she hadn't seen one copy of *her* book anywhere.

'Two weeks?' Anna looked back over the half of the resort visible from the terrace and swallowed. There was no way they would be able to wait two weeks before starting the practical work. Which meant, unfamiliar as she was with a paintbrush, Anna had little choice. She was going to need to learn—and fast.

'First things first,' Anna muttered. With two cups more of her mother's excellent coffee buzzing through her veins, she was almost raring to go. First they needed a list. Lists. Lists of repairs, lists of things they needed to make the bungalows suitable for a supermodel's wedding guests, lists of everything that needed repairing. Which meant inspecting every bungalow, every path, every deckchair and table, the beach bars, the tennis courts… She needed another list of all the lists she needed to make.

She left Sancia in the kitchen checking all the crockery for chips, dents and suspicious stains, glad of the solitude after spending a whole morning alone with her mother for the first time in more years than Anna could remember. The hotel used to be so vibrant; filled with her grandparents, their long-time staff, visitors and guests. Now it was a ghost of its old self, just one cleaner, one groundsman and a cook in residence, a couple of maids journeying over from the mainland. No guests at all. Anna suppressed a shiver. It was too quiet. Maybe she would head over to the mainland today after all, even if she only went to the small village just a few hundred metres away across the narrow strip of sea to have lunch.

The island wasn't very big, less than a mile from one end to the next, and it didn't take Anna long to reach the sheltered beach overlooking the mainland. Palms fringed the delicate yellow sand and Anna paused, taking in a deep breath, tasting the salt of sea, the lemon wafting over from the citrus trees. The sea was so blue it almost hurt, a deep turquoise that tugged at her, enticing her closer and closer. She shucked off her shoes, stepping onto the soft sand, wiggling her toes into the warm grains. When had she last been barefooted outside? Holding out her arms, she closed her eyes, feeling the sun penetrating every atom, every cell, warming her straight to her bones. The dark hair and olive skin she had inherited from her mother never really felt warm enough in Oxford; they craved this contact with the Mediterranean sun, even an early May sun better than none.

She took another deep breath, her bones aching as they absorbed the longed-for heat, inhaling the scents that always conjured up the island. For the first time in a long while she felt as if she was home.

She jumped, pulled back to the job at hand as the sound of a vacuum cleaner buzzed through the air. She wasn't on holiday, she was here to help her mother—and more importantly she was here to forget her troubles. A month away from her classes, from her research, from expectations, might give her overtired mind the reboot it so desperately needed.

Anna pulled out her notebook. She might as well start off by checking the seaworthiness of the boats. The jetty was in the next cove along, situated by the natural rock harbour, which separated the gentle, sheltered mainland-facing beaches from the more rugged sea-facing ones. The wide wooden jetty housed all the small kayaks and rowing boats kept for guests who wanted to venture out in the safe strip of sea.

Pushing her refreshed feet back into her pumps, Anna followed the narrow path as it wound round the corner and past the trees until, pushing her way through a particularly overgrown fern, she emerged, blinking, onto the boardwalk, her hair falling over her eyes.

What is that? She skidded to a stop, staring at the jetty in disbelief. In addition to several kayaks pulled high onto the pebbly beach and the boats moored tightly to the wooden posts, a white and chrome boat sat proudly in the deeper water. It was large enough to be an ocean-going boat, but this was no practical craft. Every gleaming rail, every white sail, every fitting she could see screamed 'rich man's toy' at her.

An equally gleaming dinghy was tied onto the jetty, a clear sign that someone had come ashore.

The island was private property, but occasionally day-trippers or passing boats did stop—and if they had money to spend were usually welcome. Anna looked around. She hadn't seen anyone on the main path. *'Hola!'* she called. 'Hello. Can I help you?'

No answer.

She hesitated. The sign on the jetty clearly instructed visitors—in six different languages—to head straight along the main path to Reception. Not that there was anyone actually on Reception...

'Dammit, as if I don't have enough to do.' What was her mother thinking? How could she possibly think a staff of four enough to get the island into shape for the season, let alone prepare for the wedding of the year? Sancia's airy assurances that she had enough seasonal staff ready to start soon rang hollow. They should be here by now, painting, cleaning and making sure the island was in tip-top condition.

Swivelling, Anna looked around, sucking in her breath as she saw a tall, broad figure casually strolling around the nearest bungalow, peering in through the shutters as if he had every right to be there. She thrust her shoulders back, indignation filling her. The signs were quite clear—this was private property. Without stopping to think twice she marched over to the bungalow by the straightest possible route, pushing her way through the overgrown trees and shrubs, barely noticing the branches scratching her skin.

'Excuse me.' Her Spanish completely escaped her as she reached hailing distance of the bungalow. 'What on earth do you think you're doing?'

Indignation had carried her within touching distance before common sense reasserted itself and she stopped abruptly, catching her breath as she took in the intruder. This was no over-entitled, overweight businessman out for a gentle sail. This was a pirate. Over six feet of muscled pirate. There wasn't an inch of fat—no, not a centimetre of fat—on him; his bare torso, exposed by his open white shirt, could have served as the model for Michelangelo's David. His dark hair was cropped short, his even darker eyes raking her up and down with an arrogance that made her tremble with rage.

Rage and awareness of just how grubby she was, no make-up, a crumpled old T-shirt, hair bundled hastily up. She resisted the urge to straighten her top, to shake out her hair and did her best to ignore the zing that shot straight through her traitorous body as his gaze travelled over her.

'Doing? I'm wondering if this is a hotel or a film set for a disaster movie,' he replied in heavily accented English.

'We haven't finished preparing for the opening of the season yet,' she said as loftily as she could, the heat mounting in her cheeks at the contempt in the dark depths of his eyes.

'Finished? You haven't even started. I don't know what kind of scam you're running here, *señorita*, but my sister will not be part of it.'

'Your sister?'

'Rest assured she will find somewhere else for her wedding.' He turned, his business clearly done, setting off along the overgrown path leading back to the jetty.

Anna's brain tried to unscramble the words. The big wedding, the model, the event that had sent her mother into such a spin she had summoned both her daughters to her side, the event her mother was counting on to restore the hotel's fortunes. The mess the island was in might be down to her mother's mismanagement, but how could Anna let the idyllic playground of her childhood, her beloved grandparents' legacy, fade away? Whoever this man was she had to try and persuade him not to give up on the island. 'You're the bride's brother?'

He barely paused. *'Sí.'*

Casting a look around for help and coming up blank, Anna realised with a sinking heart that it was up to her to persuade him not to tell his sister to cancel the booking. Breaking into a light jog, she followed him up the path, breathlessly braking as she reached his side. 'Look, *señor*, I know the island is in a bit of a state, but, I promise you, it will be perfect for your sister's wedding.'

Halting, he turned a scathing look on her. 'How? You have an army of elves?'

'No. No army.' How did one get an army of elves? Maybe some could write her book for her while they were here. 'We're a little behind, I admit, but I always meet my deadlines, *señor*, and this is no different. Give us the opportunity and I promise your sister will have the wedding of her dreams.'

Her words echoed round her head. 'I always meet my deadlines', her stomach lurching with the same sickening jolt it always gave when she thought about her agent's increasingly urgent emails. But she held her head high and met his thoughtful gaze, that same unwanted zing zipping through her body as his attention focussed on her. 'Please,' she said again, not too proud to beg, holding her breath while she waited for him to reply. 'Just give me a chance to prove it to you.'

* * *

Leo stared at the tall woman as she stood imploringly opposite him, hands clasped before her. He'd been surprised when she'd spoken to him in English, her accent so clear cut she could only be a native of that damp island. With her thick mass of dark hair and clear olive skin she looked like some kind of mythological Mediterranean nymph, her eyes, fringed with long dark lashes, the colour of the sea, her lips the pink of a summer sunset.

'Are you the owner?' Not that it made any difference. He needed to get back to the boat, phone Valentina and warn her this venue was a no go.

It wasn't as if his half-sister had no other choices for her wedding. Her fiancé's mother had offered the couple her Victorian house on Martha's Vineyard, but his sister had nixed that suggestion in no uncertain terms. 'She wants to make the wedding all *preppy* and tasteful,' she'd complained, scorn in her voice. Valentina's brand was all about exuberance and she wanted to make sure her wedding reflected that—and what Valentina wanted she usually got. That determination had propelled her from part-time model and socialite to online queen and super-model. Her willingness to share every instant of her life, complete with the perfect filter and hashtag, was partly what had elevated her above all the other pretty-girl wannabes, but it was hard work and a cool business brain that had turned her into a global brand.

Leo didn't understand how Valentina could bear to live her life through millions of screens, but he didn't have to. All he wanted was for her to be happy, to make up for her childhood, for the neglect from his side of her family. Which was why, after he'd heard that a fire had de-stroyed her previous choice of wedding venue, he offered to head to La Isla Marina and check out why they could accommodate a lavish wed-ding at such short notice.

It had taken approximately five seconds to reach an answer. The island was completely un-suitable—and yet here he still was. Gaze still fixed on the sea nymph, feet still fixed to the ground, still wondering exactly what shade of pink her plump lips were.

'No, I'm not the owner, I'm her daughter.

Look. I know it doesn't seem like it, but everything is under control.'

But her eyes couldn't quite meet his as she said
the words. Leo folded his arms and regarded her
sardonically, watching the faint blush of colour
spread over her cheeks. 'You're an experienced
wedding planner? Or maybe you're an events
co-ordinator? A hotel manager? A plumber and
builder? All of the above?'

She blinked. 'Well, no...'

'No? What do you do?'

'I'm a lecturer, I don't see...'

'A lecturer? In plumbing?'

Her colour heightened. 'In European history. I
mostly look at history from a feminist perspec-
tive...' She caught his eye and stopped.

'That will be very useful, I'm sure. I don't
think I need to see any more.' There was no point
in staying, no matter how pretty the help. He
turned, ready to leave when his phone buzzed.
He pulled it out. Valentina. *'Hola.'*

'Is it amazing? I wish I could be there with
you. I have to fly to Japan tomorrow, and then
I'm off to Australia for a week and there's a
shoot booked in here in New York after that

so it's impossible for me to get there before the wedding, but, Leo darling, I am so grateful that you are there making sure everything is perfect. Is it perfect? Just as I remember?'

'Valentina.' He tried to interrupt her, but his sister babbled on.

'This feels right, Leo. It is such a shame about the villa, but I spent such happy summers on La Isla Marina, that has to be a good omen, doesn't it? It will be like coming home in some ways. Todd won't know what's hit him,' she added. 'I know the Vineyard is beautiful, but I want this wedding to reflect me, to be as un-New York as possible.'

Leo paused. Valentina was extremely well off now, and she was marrying into serious old New York money, but she had been brought up on the edge of poverty thanks to his father's nasty habit of discarding his mistresses and their offspring as soon as their demands got too inconvenient. While Leo had been brought up in the solitary, austere luxury of the *castillo*, she had spent her childhood years in a tiny apartment in the rougher side of the city. Who could blame her for wanting to live the fairy tale she'd been denied? She was the daughter of a *conde* after all, even if the illustrious Lord refused to acknowledge her.

Leo looked around, assessing the island with fresh eyes. It was battered, sure, but it didn't need a fortune to bring it up to scratch; it needed some time and care. Leo could easily make that happen. It could be his wedding gift to the sister he had spent too many years not knowing. 'It needs some work, but nothing that can't be easily fixed. Don't panic.'

'How can I panic when you're there taking care of things for me, *mi hermano*? Will you keep an eye on it until I can get there? I don't need it to be perfect for the sponsors or all the people who will be watching and judging. I just want it to be perfect for me. For Todd.'

'It will be,' Leo promised. He snapped his phone shut. His options were clear: find his sister another whimsical Spanish island wedding venue able and willing to accommodate over one hundred bright young things in a month's time or make sure this place was transformed into the venue of her dreams. Besides, what else did he have to do? He fixed the nymph with a hard stare. 'Pass me that notebook,' he said. 'We have a lot of work to do.'

CHAPTER TWO

THE NYMPH CLUTCHED her notebook tightly and glared. 'We?'

'We,' Leo confirmed. 'Right now this hotel is only fit for a Halloween-themed wedding. I'm sure your knowledge of European feminist history will be very useful when it comes to sorting out the dripping showers, but just in case it isn't I am intending to stay and oversee.'

'Really?' The bright blue eyes were hard. 'And *you* know how to fix a dripping tap, I suppose?'

'I can fix a tap, tile a wall, paint woodwork. Can you?' It was all true, not that many people knew that. It would ruin his carefully cultivated, trust-funded euro-playboy image if anyone knew just how handy he was with a spanner, just as no one knew that every penny that slipped so seemingly carelessly through his fingers he had earnt. His father had cut him off at eighteen expecting a repentant and obedient son to beg for the purse strings to be reinstated. He was still waiting.

It drove him mad, not having the financial control he yearned for over his son, drove him to distraction that he had no idea where or how Leo obtained the funds for his extravagant lifestyle. And the lifestyle he saw his only son, the future Conde de Olvares, choose to lead drove him craziest of all. Every photo of Leo at another party, in a new casino, with a new model on his arm guaranteed it, Leo made sure of that. In the Conde de Olvares's rulebook appearances were everything, vices were to be hidden away.

Leo had taken his father's rule and reversed it. Every vice on the surface for everyone to see, the virtues hidden far beneath. Truth was he barely attended any parties any more—and when he did usually stayed just long enough to be photographed. Valentina had taught him well. Perception was everything.

The nymph tilted her chin defiantly. 'I'm sure I can learn. I can follow instructions.'

'That's good to know,' Leo said softly and her cheeks burned a deeper red.

'Look. I can see why you're worried.' Her gaze

slid over to the nearest bungalow. 'But I have assured you, repeatedly, that everything is under control.'

Leo followed her gaze. The bungalow was dirty, the white paint peeling off the external walls, the trees and flowers growing so close it was only a matter of time till nature recolonised the building. It needed nails in the roof, a lick of paint and a damn good clean. Hot, sweaty, hard manual work.

His eyes narrowed. Maybe the work would help fix the melancholy he couldn't quite shake. Leo wasn't sure he'd ever experienced real, unadulterated happiness, but for the past twelve years he had managed something resembling content; always on the move, always making money, always his own man. But ever since Valentina had announced her engagement, that contentment had become elusive, her glowing happiness a sharp contrast to his darkness.

Leo had always thought that they were cut from the same cloth, but now his baby sister was proving braver—or more foolhardy—than him. Either way Leo was left in her wake. It was an uncomfortable place to be.

His original intention had been to make a few phone calls and get a team of labourers despatched to La Isla Marina then return in a month's time to enjoy the wedding, but maybe a few weeks getting his hands dirty on a beautiful island with a beautiful girl was exactly what he needed. Time out from his usual regime.

Turning, he held out his hand. 'Leo di Marquez y Correa,' he said and braced himself. There was no flare of recognition in her blue eyes, no rise of her straight, no nonsense brows. Nearly everyone Leo met had already formed an opinion of him. Most people either disapproved of him, wanted to party with him or wanted to sleep with him. A very few, those in the know, wanted his investment. He rarely, however, met with blank politeness bordering on disdain.

It would be an interesting challenge to turn that disdain to desire. His blood stirred at the very thought; he did have a few weeks with no plans after all...

'Anna Gray,' she said after a moment, making no move to take his hand. 'Dr Anna Gray.'

'A doctor as well as an expert on feminism in Europe's history?' He smiled to show he was joking, turning on the full force of his charm to see if he could tempt those pink lips to smile.

She didn't respond in kind, folding her arms defensively. 'I have a PhD from Oxford, not that it's any of your business. Look, Señor di Marquez…'

'Leo.'

'I appreciate that things look a little ramshackle right now, and I know your sister's wedding is going to get a lot of publicity…'

'Publicity which will benefit you.'

'But I assure you, we are quite capable of getting everything ready in plenty of time…'

'Then I'm very sure another pair of hands will come in very useful. I'll make it easy for you, Dr Gray. I'll sleep on my boat and work for food alone. I won't even tell my sister just how much needs to be done here. Tell me, are you really in a position to refuse?'

Anna hugged her notebook tighter, her mind working furiously. She should be snatching Leo's offer with both hands, but something held her back. She didn't know whether it was the sardonic look in his dark eyes, the smirk playing about his mouth or the teasing tone in his voice. It didn't help that he was one of the most insanely handsome men she had ever seen in the flesh. Oxford wasn't exactly short of over-confident men thinking they could win using their charm alone, but the city didn't run to Spanish pirates, nor was she used to conducting conversations with practically bare-chested men.

It also didn't help that her knees weakened every time he fixed that intense gaze on her, that she could feel her pulse speeding up faster and faster. Her friends had been telling her to get out and date more. This must be her body's way of agreeing if one hard-eyed, hard-chested man could have this effect on her.

Anna dragged her thoughts away from Leo's chest and back to the matter at hand, her eyes narrowing as she considered his far-too-good-to-be-true offer. 'Don't you have a job to go to? How will you manage to take a month off work with no notice?'

'I work for myself and I am a famously forgiving boss.'

Lucrative boss if that boat was anything to

judge by. 'It's not up to me,' Anna said finally. 'My mother owns the island.'

'Then lead on. I'll present my credentials to your leader.'

Anna tried to hold his amused gaze, but to her frustration her own dropped first. She could stand up in front of a full lecture theatre without breaking a sweat, turn overly confident undergraduates into shaking shadows of their former selves with one disbelieving arch of an eyebrow, but in front of this man her defences crumbled. 'Fine,' she said tightly. 'Follow me.'

As she led him along the overgrown paths, Anna was aware of Leo's keen gaze taking in every crack, every break in the path and the surrounding buildings and worry shivered through her once again. Had the resort been on the road to such dilapidation when her grandparents were still alive? They had been pretty old, after all, their staff of a similar age. It would have been too easy for things to start to slide unnoticed by them. Her mother, though, had little excuse. She'd been living here for nearly a decade, ever since she had drifted away from the family home for a holiday, a holiday that bled into an extended stay, which in turn became a separation. The same old frustration bubbled up and Anna curled her hands into loose fists. No doubt her mother had just employed her usual mantra of *mañana*, never worrying that one day she would have to deal with the rapidly escalating problems.

Well, she wasn't dealing, was she? Anna was here dealing for her. As usual.

Only, who was she to cast aspersions? Wasn't she doing exactly the same thing with her book? Hoping that somehow something miraculous would happen and it would all fall into place. Running away from her problems…

'So tell me, what does being a Professor of European history with a feminist slant entail these days?' Anna started, guiltily. It was as if Leo had read her mind. 'You seem very young to be a professor.'

'You're not the first to say that.' Although most people also snidely insinuated her renowned historian father had helped her climb the academic ladder faster than usual, that her name was responsible for her success, not her credentials. Or they looked down at the success of her first book, convinced a popular history book couldn't be as well-researched, as important, as an academic paper read only by other specialists in her field. It had been easier to hold her head high when she hadn't doubted herself, when she had been sure that the academic life was all she needed.

'I'm sure I'm not. Is it all libraries and lectures?'

'Mostly,' she admitted. 'There's a huge pressure to publish papers as well as teach.'

'And do you?'

'Papers, books. A book,' she amended, trying not to think about the mess that was book number two.

'An author? How impressive. Would I have read your book?'

'Only if you're interested in a rehabilitation of Joanna the Mad from a feminist standpoint, looking at how difficult it was for intelligent women to thrive in a male-dominated world.'

'I definitely missed that one. Joanna the Mad? Is she the one who carted her dead husband's body all over Spain?'

'That's one of the myths my book works to dispel.'

'Pity, I've always felt that if I got married I'd want my wife to love me enough to keep my corpse by her side at all times.' Anna shot him a quick glance. Joanna's husband had been famously known as Philip the Handsome, but surely even he would have paled into plainness next to the rugged good looks of Leo di Marquez. She caught his eye and felt her cheeks heat up yet again. What on earth was wrong with her? She'd never been a blusher before. If she carried on at this rate they could save money on an electrician and use her face as a lamp.

To Anna's relief they finally reached the villa. Leo looked at the ornate, white building, more like a Moorish palace than a hotel reception and office, and whistled. 'Nice.'

Despite herself Anna felt the old ripples of pride. As a child she had always felt so special, so chosen, to be part of the island's heritage, to spend her summers in her little turret room surveying the island like some kind of medieval queen. 'It's not as old as it looks. It's a turn-of-the-last-century reproduction built by my great-grandfather as a wedding gift for his bride,' she explained. 'This was their own private island, but when my grandfather inherited, he couldn't afford to keep it as a second home. He and my grandmother turned the island into a resort. At one time, back in the fifties, this was one of the most exclusive resorts in the Mediterranean.' Anna looked up at the veranda's cobweb-infested ceiling and tried not to sigh. It was hard to imagine the island in its glamorous heyday right now.

'And now?'

'It's been a while since I visited,' Anna admitted. 'Things are a little less glamorous than they used to be.'

The problem was the island was expensive to run. Her grandfather had often bemoaned the price of labour and food, all of which needed shipping out; the mainland might be just a few hundred metres away, but the island was still only accessible by boat. Maybe they needed to think differently, turn the island into an event destination rather than a hotel, for weddings and other special occasions?

They? She pursed her lips. There was no way her mother would be capable of running that kind of business, and it was unlikely Rosa would want to stay in one place and help. Maybe, much as the idea broke Anna's heart, her mother should sell the island to someone who could look after it.

She'd broach the subject after the wedding. There was no point getting embroiled in a family drama before.

She led Leo through the grand hallway, now a hotel reception area, a board behind the huge desk holding the big iron keys that still unlocked the bungalow doors—no flimsy key cards here—and along the wooden panelled hallway until they reached the vast kitchen where her mother was still sorting crockery.

'*Mama?*'

Piles of brightly painted terracotta plates, bowls and cups covered every surface and most of the floor. In the middle of the chaos Sancia stood swaying, her hair falling out of its customary loose bun, her eyes closed as she sang along to the ear-piercingly loud music blaring from the radio. Anna winced, unable to even glance in Leo's direction.

The scene was all too reminiscent, a flashback to her teenage years. She'd soon stopped bringing friends home, no idea what would greet them once they walked through the front door into the untidy hallway. Sancia was usually at home, but she would be preoccupied with her current fad; dancing, painting, sculpting, cooking. Whatever it was tended to take over the whole house, a chaotic tangle of colour and mess. It was all about the creative journey, Sancia would say, whenever Anna or her father suggested she keep her artistic endeavours confined to one room. Which was a good thing as usually the end result was good for nothing at all. Anna preferred to spend her after-school time at her friends' houses instead, in ordered, peaceful homes where everything had its place and routines ruled.

'Mama!' she said again, this time loudly and sharply, and Sancia's eyes flew open, fastening onto her daughter reproachfully.

'*Querida*, there is no need to shout.' She switched her gaze over to Leo and her dark eyes widened, her still-full mouth curving into a smile. '*Hola.*'

Anna's heart sank; she recognised that particular flirtatious smile. It was her mother's default smile for any reasonably attractive man and Anna had seen it used, always to great effect, on friends of her father's, and on her own friends' fathers. No girl should have to grow up seeing grown men reduced to red-faced boys by her own mother. Anna knew it wasn't conscious, that warm smile of appreciation, it wasn't meant with malice or intent or even deliberate flirtatiousness, but it was all the more devastating for that.

Leo didn't seem to be immune, his own smile wide as he bent over Sancia's outstretched hand. *'Hola,'* he answered, his voice so low it was a cross between a purr and a growl, a deep rumble Anna suspected was used as often as her mother's smile and with a similar effect—only she was pretty sure Leo di Marquez knew exactly what he was doing.

Sancia preened. 'Who is your charming *amigo*, Anna?'

Anna made a concerted effort not to grind her teeth. 'Mama, this is Señor di Marquez, he is Valentina's brother and he's come to check the island is suitable for his sister's wedding.'

Sancia turned her smile up another watt. 'What a lucky girl to have such an involved brother.'

She gazed up at Leo as if he were edible and Anna tried not to follow her mother's gaze, especially as she seemed fixated on Leo's half-bared chest.

'Your resort is beautiful, *señora*,' Leo said, a smile still playing around his beautifully sculpted mouth.

'*Gracias*, and please, call me Sancia. *Señora* always makes me feel so old. I trust you're happy with everything? We are so looking forward to welcoming Valentina and her fiancé in a month's time.'

Anna stared at her mother in disbelief. Did she really think anyone would be *happy* with the state of the island? After all, it wasn't as if she didn't know what a huge task she had in front of her—she had called both her daughters to beg them to drop everything to come and help. Maybe now Anna was here Sancia considered her own job done. She had always relied on Anna to look after the dreary practicalities in the past. 'That's my sensible, organised girl,' she would say, as if sensible and organised were things to be tolerated, to be pitied, not to emulate.

By the way Leo's mouth quirked he was evidently amused by Sancia's blind optimism. 'Obviously you are not quite ready for the season,' he said. Why was he being so diplomatic with Sancia when he hadn't minced one of his words with Anna? 'As you know Valentina needs everything to be perfect and so I have promised to help you prepare the island for her wedding. I trust this is acceptable?'

If Sancia's eyes grew any wider they would fall right out of her head. As it was she was currently resembling a cartoon character more than a real human being. 'That is so kind of you.'

Anna couldn't stop her toe tapping impatiently on the tiled floor. Was her mother going to look at this practically in any way? Check that Leo was who he said he was, that Valentina wanted his input and, most importantly, that his presence here for a month wouldn't result in any reduction of the lavish payment Valentina had offered in return for a week's exclusivity? She took her mother's arm and steered her through the piles of bowls and plates to the open back door, lowering her voice and doing her best to ignore Leo's sardonic glance. 'Mama, don't you think you should check with your client first, and make sure this doesn't mean there will be any renegotiation on the price? That Leo is who he says he is.' But she knew she was wasting her breath.

'*Querida*, the fates have brought you a handsome young man and you want to check his references? Live a little, Anna. You're getting hunched, all that time over a keyboard, and you look positively sallow. A few weeks in the sunshine with some agreeable company is exactly what you need.'

'I'm not here for my health, Mama. I'm here to help you...'

'And thanks to Señor di Marquez your job will be a lot easier. After all, Anna, you're not the most practical of people, are you?' And while the gobsmacked Anna was still trying to formulate an articulate response her mother stepped away, turning back to Leo. 'We have plenty of space here in the villa, Señor di Marquez. I would be very happy to accommodate you.'

'Señor di Marquez has his own accommodation,' Anna interjected quickly.

Her mother's smile barely wavered. 'But we will feed you, I insist, it's the least I can do.

Lunch will be served in just a couple of hours so shall we meet back here at two? I'm really looking forward to getting to know you better.'

Uh-oh. Anna knew exactly what that meant. At least four courses, wine and two hours of the day wasted. Then, no doubt, her mother would suggest a siesta and before Anna had had a chance to make even one list the day would be over. 'There's no need for a formal lunch. There's far too much to do. We can easily just grab a roll and some cheese and work through. It's only early May. It's not as if the sun will be too unbearable,' she finished a little doubtfully as she glanced out of the window at the perfectly blue, cloudless sky.

'Oh, Anna...' Her mother couldn't have sounded more reproachful if Anna had suggested drowning kittens, but her sorrowful protestation was drowned out by Leo, who leaned against the huge scrubbed table, arms folded and a sardonic gleam in his eyes.

'Skip lunch? Absolutely not. I'm looking forward to it, *señora*—I mean, Sancia. What's life without time out for good food and good conversation?'

Narrowing her eyes, Anna stared over at the insouciant Spaniard. 'I thought you wanted everything to be perfect for your sister's wedding?'

'I do, it will be, but there's no reason we can't have a little fun while we're working, now, is there?'

CHAPTER THREE

LEO TOOK A small sip of his coffee and grinned over at Anna. She had become increasingly, obviously impatient as lunch had meandered from course to course: fish soup followed by an excellent soufflé, chicken with garlic-roasted potatoes, and a cheese course, all washed down with a rather good rioja. Sancia Garcia might not know how to run a hotel, but she did know how to employ a good cook and right now, sitting on a sheltered patio with a view of white beaches and an azure-blue sea, Leo felt a stir of that elusive contentment for the first time in months.

Sure, there was an entire island to be renovated and made fit for Valentina's arrival in just under a month, but the sense of urgency was lessened by the rich dark coffee, the richer wine and the last sliver of cheese temptingly within reach. Lessened by the knowledge he could make a phone call and an army of labourers would be despatched forth to take care of every detail. But mostly lessened by Dr Anna Gray's palatable disapproval. She had only eaten soup and a little cheese, had refused wine and was very obviously making copious lists proving just how busy she really was.

It was quite adorable. Not that Leo looked for adorable in women. He didn't really look for anything beyond the very, very superficial. What was the point when he had no intention of getting into anything deeper than casual? He chose carefully, ensuring the women he dated were as uninterested in his inner life as he was in theirs. He needed to be sure that they wouldn't be looking too closely at him. Too closely into him. That all they were interested in was his blue blood and deep pockets.

Of course here, out of the public eye, the usual rules didn't apply. It would be an interesting challenge to see just what it took to make Dr Anna Gray put down her pen and notepad, wipe those frown lines off her forehead and smile. Interesting, but all too risky. He'd known Anna for less than three hours and he already knew that she was the type who would always dig deeper—and that made her dangerous. Besides, he was pretty sure she didn't understand the 'good time' rule and *that* made her absolutely off-limits.

'Hit me.' He pushed his coffee cup to one side, propping his elbows on the table as he turned towards Anna. 'What's first?'

Anna brushed a lock of dark hair away from her forehead and Leo froze, awareness of her every movement shivering through him. For one endless second she was imprinted on him, her long graceful neck, her sweep of long, wavy hair, the shrewd expression in her clear blue eyes, and the vulnerability he saw behind them, a vulnerability he sensed was usually kept well hidden.

'First?'

Leo nodded at the notebook Anna carried like a talisman. 'On your list.'

'Oh.' Her hand lay over the page protectively. 'I've put together a list of supplies we need before we can really get started so I think I need to take a trip over to the mainland today. There really isn't any time to waste.' She glared meaningfully at his plate. 'Mama, I'll need to take your dinghy. Is that okay? Is the car still kept in the same place?'

'No need to borrow your mother's boat. I'll sail you over.' Leo sat back in his chair and watched Anna try and come up with an excuse to avoid his company.

Anna blinked. 'There's no point taking your boat such a short distance.'

'No, but my dinghy is at your dock.'

Sancia glanced from Leo to Anna, her expression amused. 'The car is parked in the harbour lot as always, *querida*. There's a big store on the outskirts of town, about five kilometres from the harbour. You can't miss it.'

'Right.' Anna pushed her chair back and stood up. 'Let's go.'

Leo didn't move.

She tapped her foot, her eyes gleaming dangerously. 'In your own time, *señor.*'

Sancia sighed, shaking her head at her daughter. '*Querida*, you are in Spain now. The store will be closed for siesta. There's no point in going now.'

'A siesta sounds like an excellent suggestion.' Leo winked at Anna. 'I'll see you at the jetty in two hours, Dr Gray. Bring your lists.' And he stood up. 'Thank you, Sancia, that was delicious.' He bowed over Sancia's hand and tossed another wink in Anna's direction before sauntering away, fully aware that Anna was glaring at him. His back prickled with awareness; he could almost feel the burn as her eyes bored into him.

Funny to think he had had no agenda this morning beyond popping over to what he had assumed to be a perfectly run luxury resort in order to reassure his sister. Now he had a month's work ahead of him and a hostile colleague. He couldn't wait to get started.

Anna stared down at the bucket of tepid, dirty water resentfully. She'd decided not to waste the two hours her mother and Leo were choosing to spend sleeping and instead had got started scrubbing down the outside of a couple of bungalows. Not that she had got very far. Right now getting the island into any kind of order seemed like a Sisyphean task—especially if long lunches and longer siestas were going to be the order of the day.

Still, at least she had made a start. She would get the groundskeeper and chambermaid to continue while she was on the mainland; but she really needed to talk to her mother and find out when the seasonal staff were due to start, and how many they were expecting. Without adequate staffing they would never get the island ready in time. Luckily the interiors of the bungalows were in a better state than she'd expected. They needed some cosmetic work, a good clean, taps and showers fixing, a quick paint, but the furniture was still good, simple, but well-crafted. A few luxurious touches, new cushions, rugs and accessories should bring them up to date. After all, if Valentina wanted marble and gilt she would have booked a hotel. She was after an authentic Spanish touch and that, at least, La Isla Marina could provide.

Picking up the bucket, Anna tipped the water down the drain. She'd worked her way through several buckets of water, lugging them to the desired spot, sloshing water down her legs as she did so. Her hands were red, two nails already broken. She made a mental note to add gloves to her list.

Had it really only been half an hour of work? It felt like eternity and she had barely started. This morning she'd been full of a sense of purpose, if a little daunted. Now she just felt like Cinderella, toiling away while the rest of the household slumbered, and just because she had volunteered for domestic drudgery didn't mean she couldn't help feeling resentful. She wouldn't mind so much if Rosa weren't swanking about somewhere, carefree, on the other side of the world, if her mother didn't look at her as if she were being fussy, if Leo di Marquez hadn't shown up...

Anna pushed her hair off her forehead, grimacing as she realised just how sweaty she was. What was Leo's deal anyway? What kind of man just decided to put a month aside for his sister's wedding with no planning, no notice? Placing the bucket on the floor, Anna tried to stop her mind dwelling on the planes of Leo's chest, the strong, sensual mouth, his mocking eyes. He knew how attractive he was all right—and there was nothing Anna distrusted more than a man convinced of his own worth, his own desirability. After all, she'd been taken in before, been badly burnt before.

She'd mishandled him from the first, allowing him to put her on the back foot even though he was the trespasser. It wouldn't—couldn't—happen again. She needed weapons, she needed armour, she needed control, she needed facts.

Her mother and sister might rely on intuition and spontaneity, but there was much more comfort in knowledge and plans. That was why she had become an academic, not because of her father's pre-eminence or because it was expected of her, but because she liked to dig deep, to find out the facts, to draw her own interpretation. If Leo's sister was some kind of media star then it shouldn't be too hard to find out exactly who he was, what he was. And then she would be prepared.

Mind made up, Anna headed back to the villa, letting herself through the hidden door that separated the public spaces from the family's private rooms. The wooden staircase was narrow and dark as she climbed all the way to the top floor and the turret bedroom that had been hers since she was a baby. Nothing had changed: the same iron bedstead stood in the corner, the same pictures hung on the whitewashed walls, the same colourful blankets were heaped on the bed. It was sparse and small, but Anna liked the memories of when they had been a proper family, Rosa in the other turret, her parents nearby, her grandparents still alive.

A pang of guilt hit her at the thought of her father home alone, rattling around their huge Oxford house. She'd left him a schedule, all his pills laid out ready, labelled meals in the freezer for the evenings he didn't dine in college. And she'd promised to text him reminders every day—he probably wouldn't even notice she was gone. She bit her lip, his lined, grey face clear in her mind. The only time he had ever relaxed was here on the island, when he would push his research and work aside for a few days, sometimes even weeks. When had he last taken a real holiday? Not since Sancia had left him. Left them.

Her laptop was already set up on the desk, her notebooks stacked neatly by its side, colour-coded by theme. Anna averted her eyes from the notebooks, an all too visual reminder that she still had no book, not even the bare bones of one. The usual wave of nausea swirled low in her stomach, the age-old fear that she would be revealed as an imposter, a fraud, whispering in her mind. Had she really thought that if she ran away to the island her doubts would stay meekly in Oxford? They were just as strong as ever—except when she had been engrossed in painting. Except when she had been sparring with Leo di Marquez... Pushing her notebooks to one side, she switched on her laptop, typed in Valentina's name and began to read.

Half an hour later Anna sat back and stared at the screen; she still had no idea what Valentina did or why she was famous. Sure, the curvy brunette modelled, but she'd started modelling *after* she had got famous; for all her prominence she was a little shorter, a little bustier than the usual top models. Valentina seemed to spend her time photographing herself, her friends, her clothes and her food and posting the pictures up for comment. And she received them in their thousands, more, hundreds of thousands. Anna frowned as she looked at the photo posted just this morning, a photo of breakfast laid out on a patio table, every colour popping off the screen. How on earth was this a job? Judging by the lavish apartment, the designer clothes, the parties, it was lucrative even if it made no sense.

Most of the recent posts and tweets focussed

on the forthcoming wedding. Anna's stomach clenched as she read through them; Valentina's expectations were high and the results would be instantly seen around the world. If they could make it a success then the island's fortunes would turn around overnight, but if they failed then they would fall very publicly. She had no choice; if there was to be any chance of pulling this off she simply had to work with Leo.

Except not once had she seen his name mentioned. Valentina made reference to growing up on the Barcelona coast, to working in a beach bar, to her mother, who had died a few years back—but there was no mention of a brother or a father. Not one.

Okay, then more research was needed. Anna poised her fingers over the keyboard for a second and then typed in *Leo di Marquez y Correa*.

'Bingo,' she said softly. The picture on the very first link looked very familiar indeed. The same close-cropped dark hair, the same sharp cheekbones set off by stubble too perfect to be completely natural. This Leo was dressed a lot more formally, in a light grey suit, a smiling blonde in a skin-tight dress hanging off his arm. Anna read the caption. 'Leo's new model'. Hmmm, it looked as if he was as at home in the gossip pages as his sister.

'He's not a pirate, he's a playboy,' she muttered as she brought up article after article. Leo on his boat, bare-chested in the sun, Leo in a casino, on a superyacht surrounded by the most glamorous people Anna had ever seen, Leo spraying champagne. Her stomach tightened. 'Spoilt, rich boys.' She could taste the contempt, bitter on her tongue.

The facts were there in clear black and white. Not just spoilt, not just rich, but Spanish aristocracy. The only son—only child—of the Conde de Olvares, a haughty grey-haired man, and his even haughtier-looking wife, Leo had been a fixture on the party scene since he was eighteen years old. No job, no occupation beyond sailing, gambling, drinking and women.

Anna stood up and stalked over to the window. From her vantage point high in the tower she could see the jetty and the gleaming boat moored out in the sea. A boat he hadn't worked to buy, a toy for a pampered princeling. Disappointment twisted her chest and she had no idea why. She didn't know Leo, and it wasn't as if she had liked what she had seen after all. Well, not beyond the physical at least. It was just she hadn't expected anything quite this shallow.

Anna knew the type all too well. They weren't as prevalent at Oxford as they had once been, but there were still plenty of entitled lordlings, their places secured by their name, their lineage, their education, their futures assured no matter what. They didn't care what anyone thought about them, didn't care what the consequences of their actions might be. At eighteen she might have been stupid enough to mistake that arrogant confidence for magnetism, found the frivolity and extravagance glamorous, but not any more. Now she valued work, reliability, sense. Old-fashioned values maybe, but her values.

And not only was Leo di Marquez a playboy, he was a liar. Valentina wasn't his sister, he was an only child. So what on earth was he doing here?

Of course he was late. Anna had known he would be and yet she had still arrived at the jetty at the agreed time, her shorts swapped for light cotton trousers, her T-shirt for a loose shirt, her notebook tucked away in a waterproof bag.

She'd deliberated sailing across alone and not waiting for Leo, but she wanted answers. Nothing added up. Why did a party playboy want to spend a month doing DIY on a tiny island with barely any inhabitants, no nightlife, no fun? And why had he claimed Valentina was his sister when she clearly wasn't?

She squinted over to the boat, lounging out in the flat sea like the embodiment of entitlement, blowing out a frustrated breath when she saw a tall figure swing over the side and climb down to the dinghy bobbing alongside. *Finally.*

It didn't take her long to walk to the end of the jetty, arriving there just as Leo executed a perfect, stylish turn to bring the small open boat alongside. 'Hop in,' he called. 'Unless you need me to help you?' He held out a hand, which Anna ignored as she stepped gingerly into the boat, seating herself at the furthest end away from Leo. He barely waited until she was seated before releasing the throttle and, with a roar, the boat sped off towards the mainland.

Despite her trepidation Anna found herself relaxing on the short trip, leaning against the back rail enjoying the sun on her face, the splash of the water on her outstretched hand as the boat cut through the sea. In Oxford, she saw students punting or kayaking all the time and yet never made time to get out onto the water herself, which was odd when she remembered just what a water baby she had always been on the island; surfing, windsurfing, boating, swimming until her skin wrinkled, her hair thick with salt.

Steering the boat towards the public harbour, Leo found a mooring spot right next to the main jetty. Small boats bobbed all around, larger cruisers and yachts moored further out in the deeper water. Anna could see the perfect curve of the beach to one side, deserted despite the sun, and the cheerful fronts of the bars and restaurants that lined the shore road behind it. Cala del Mar had seemed like the height of sophistication when Anna was in her teens. Now she saw it as the sleepy, provincial seaside village it was, all the fonder of it for its simplicity.

Leo killed the engine then turned and eyed Anna quizzically as she stayed seated, making no attempt to climb out of the boat. 'Are you stuck?'

'Why are you here?'

'That's a very philosophical question. Why are any of us here?' But the laughter drained out of his dark eyes despite the easy smile on his face.

'You know what I mean. Why have you decided to stay on the island? Why announce your intention of helping? What does the son of the Conde de Olvares want with a tiny island resort? There's no casino, no nightclub, no supermodels to entertain you.'

'Someone's been doing her homework.' The smile still played around his mouth, but there was an edge to his voice.

Anna raised her chin. 'It's all a matter of public record, as is the fact you're an only child. So why did you tell me Valentina was your sister?'

The smile disappeared, his eyes hardening to flints. 'Because she is. And she wants the perfect wedding and I am going to make sure that happens. Any other questions, Sherlock Holmes, or shall we get on with the matter at hand?' And without looking at Anna he climbed out of the boat and started along the jetty, head high, back ramrod straight. Anna stared at the set shoulders, the jerky stride. Somehow she had touched a nerve without getting any of the answers she sought and although Leo was the one lying, or at least omitting information, Anna felt as if she was the one in the wrong.

She blew out a frustrated breath before getting carefully to her feet and stepping out of the boat onto the dusty jetty. This wasn't over and she would get her answers. Leo di Marquez was playing some kind of game and Anna wasn't going to stop until she had worked out just what he was up to.

CHAPTER FOUR

LEO STEPPED BACK and surveyed the wooden wall, an unexpected pride swelling his chest. If he said so himself it looked rather professional. Sanding, filling and painting were proving to be unexpectedly soothing, each finished wall or window frame a tangible achievement in a way a successful deal or investment no longer seemed to be. Maybe that was because money was such an abstract thing. He didn't exactly sit counting gold coins, had more than enough, even for his fairly lavish needs.

Leo put the paintbrush back on the tray and stretched before reaching for his task list, a wry grin curving his mouth as he scanned the typed list, complete with timings and required equipment. Anna had, with the help of her trusty notebook, worked out a plan. A plan, Leo had not failed to notice, which kept him at one side of the island and her at the other. Nor could he help noticing that she no longer broke for lunch, and although she joined Sancia, himself and the staff for dinner she was usually distracted, spending the meal making even more lists or researching fixtures and fittings rather than joining in the conversation. He had a strong suspicion she was avoiding him.

Como sea. Let her keep her distance. Sure, he had enjoyed the brief one-sided flirtation, had thought it might be amusing to—metaphorically at least—unbutton the terminally uptight doctor, but there were limits to even his amusement and those limits had been reached when Anna had rounded on him with a scornful expression he knew only too well. It was the same expression he saw on his parents' faces. The expression he sometimes saw in the mirror.

Still, over the last few days he had almost reached a state of contentment. It was repetitive work, this washing, sanding, filling and paint-ing, but it had an end goal. Each task added up to a whole, a newly restored bungalow. Well, an almost restored bungalow because along with the repainting of the outside Leo was making a list of all the more specialised tasks that needed doing: the dripping taps, the under-performing showers, the broken tiles, the holes in roofs.

Right now it was just he and Anna with their buckets and ladders and paintbrushes. At the start of next week they would be joined by the seasonal staff including three more grounds-men and, for a week, a plumber, a joiner and a builder. That would leave two weeks for any internal repainting, replacement of furniture and adding in all the extras Valentina and her friends would expect to find in a luxury hotel. Anna seemed to spend any time she wasn't painting flicking through lifestyle blogs and upmarket magazines, every session resulting in even more copious notes and yet another list.

The full-time groundsman and maid were equally hard at work on the public and communal areas. With three separate beach bars as well as the main bar and restaurant, two lounges and the beautiful central pagoda, where the marriage ceremony was to be carried out, they had their work cut out and Maria, the maid, was volubly looking forward to the arrival of her seasonal counterparts to help share the load. The island might shut over the winter, but it still seemed like a particularly sparse skeleton staff when the off season was surely the time to refresh and repair?

How on earth had this place survived over the last few years? Sancia swung from relaxed to mildly concerned—on the surface anyway—but Leo occasionally saw a flash of worry in the dark eyes when yet another dozen items were added to Anna's seemingly inexhaustible lists.

'Here, Sancia sent this for you.'

A soft voice pulled him away from his thoughts and Leo turned, list still in hand, to see Anna standing under the shade of the overgrown copse of trees. His breath caught. Her mass of dark hair was pulled up into a ponytail, she wasn't wearing a scrap of make-up and her cut-off denims and simple navy T-shirt were strictly utilitarian yet a quiver of attraction still ran through him.

His gaze dropped to the tray she clasped tightly in her hands. It held a plate heaped with a roll, sliced meat and fresh tomatoes and a bottle of beer.

Anna held it out towards him. 'You missed lunch.'

Leo glanced at his watch. Sure enough it was nearly three. 'I got a little carried away.'

'Obviously.' She took a step nearer, eyes crinkled as she looked critically at the walls. 'It's looking good though.'

'Does that surprise you?'

'Yes,' she said and, jolted by surprise, Leo looked at her.

'Okaaaay...' he said slowly.

'I thought you'd get bored after a couple of days, or you would spend most of your days lounging around on your boat, spend an hour with a paintbrush in your hand and expect us to fall at your feet in gratitude. But, you have more than pulled your weight.' She took a visibly deep breath. 'I was wrong.'

'*Sí.*' But he couldn't bring himself to labour the point. She had good reasons for her misconceptions, reasons Leo himself had planted. He couldn't blame her, just because for some reason he wanted her to look deeper. Wanted her to look beyond the playboy image and see what lay underneath—if anything lay beneath. He doubted it, but if there was anything there then surely Dr Anna Gray was the kind of woman to excavate it.

'So.' She hefted the tray up awkwardly. 'Are you hungry?'

He was ravenous, he realised. Nothing like sheer physical labour to get a man's appetite going. *'Sí,'* he said again, taking the tray from her and heading over to the wrought-iron patio table each bungalow was furnished with, perfect for al-fresco dining. This particular table was positioned to take advantage of the sea views and to get shelter from the midday sun and as Leo lowered himself onto the cool seat he realised how very hot and thirsty he was.

Anna shifted from foot to foot. 'Okay, then, enjoy. I'll just…'

'Join me,' he said, without realising he was going to extend the invitation. 'Unless you have a pressing appointment with a paintbrush, that is?'

She pulled a face. 'I am *dreaming* about paintbrushes.'

'Then a break is probably just what the doctor ordered.'

She hesitated for a long moment before, with a

nod, more an acknowledgement to herself than to him, she walked over to the table. 'Probably.'

As she sat herself in the other chair Leo realised this was the first time they had been alone together in nearly a week, the first time since they had gone shopping for supplies and she had called him a liar.

'I shouldn't stay too long.' She leaned forward, her head drooping into her hands, shoulders sagging in weariness. 'I want to get the bungalow I'm on finished, and then I need to go through all Valentina's plans and make sure we have ordered everything we need.'

'Anna, have you ever heard the word delegate? Do you really think you can single-handedly renovate the entire island *and* be a wedding planner?'

She looked up at that. 'Who else is there, Leo? If everything isn't perfect then the island will be ruined, completely finished. God knows, it's on its last legs as it is. But if we—if I—can pull this off then we can save the island, save my grandparents' dream.' She looked down at her hands. 'It's an incredible opportunity, but it's so daunting. This is the most public wedding of the year, people are betting on which designer is making her dress and whether Valentina will wear a veil—it's insane.

'Add in one hundred and fifty guests, all arriving at once, the wedding that very evening followed by a huge party and then a week of celebrations. It's a lot to deal with.' She heaved a gusty sigh. 'I know we still have three weeks, and thank goodness most of the seasonal staff are able to arrive a week earlier than Mama had originally asked them to, but there is still so much to do, just to make the island look presentable, let alone the actual wedding itself. Thank goodness Valentina paid a huge deposit. We need every penny.'

'What was your mother thinking? To say yes to a wedding she clearly wasn't ready for?'

Her face closed. 'She *didn't* think. She never does. She acts spontaneously and then expects someone else to sort out all the details. Me. She expects me to sort out the details while she pats my shoulder and tells me to relax and why can't I be more like my sister?'

'You have sisters?' How had he not known this?

'One sister.' Her voice was tight. 'Rosa. She's

a photographer. Travels around being all bohemian and socially conscious and doing exactly what she wants whenever she wants.'

Leo blinked, taken aback by the anger in Anna's voice—the anger and the hurt. 'You don't get on, then?' He'd always dreamed of a sibling growing up, of someone to share the burden of being a di Marquez. He adored Valentina, but they hadn't been raised together, their relationship unknown to anyone outside their immediate family—and Anna. Leo didn't know why he had blurted out the information to her. Not that it mattered; she hadn't believed him anyway.

'We're very different. Right now Rosa is on a beach somewhere in South America being artistic and free while I have taken leave from my job—my respected and important job—to help out. But when Rosa does finally waltz up, my mother will treat her like the prodigal daughter. A calf is probably being fatted right now.' The anger had faded. Now Anna just sounded sad. 'I haven't spoken to her in three years. Not since my grandfather's funeral. Much as I could do with her help, I have to admit I'm dreading her actually being here.'

Leo took a swig of the beer then pushed the bottle over to her. 'What happened?'

Taking the bottle with a faint smile, Anna set it before her, her fingers pulling at the label. 'We've always seen the world differently, never been close. Things just came to a head when I was invited to spend a semester at Harvard as a visiting teacher. Rosa was in England for a few weeks following the funeral and I asked her to stay on in Oxford while I was away It was only for a few months. Dad had—has—some heart problems. They were talking about the possibility of surgery. But she said she had her own commitments. That he was an adult. That he had to slow down and take responsibility for himself.'

'What did you do?'

'What could I do? I couldn't leave him. I said stuff, she said stuff, she left, we don't speak. That's it. Nothing exciting.'

'He's better now? You're here after all.'

'I text him every night to remind him to take his pills.' She shook her head. 'Maybe Rosa is right. Maybe I do have some kind of martyr complex. Look at me. Twenty-eight and I'm spending my leave working—unpaid and unthanked—for my mother. I spend my few leisure hours as my father's PA and carer. It's months since I went on a date, years really. I barely see my friends, spend most of my evenings working.' Her voice was so quiet he could barely hear her, her eyes fixed on the sea. He wondered if she had forgotten his very existence. 'Sometimes I wonder if this is it. This will be my life. In one way I'm so lucky, have achieved so much so young and yet even that doesn't feel right. It wouldn't matter if the new book was going well. At least I could be the academic *wunderkind*.'

Now she just looked defeated, her face almost grey, and Leo remembered how he'd felt when he first saw her. How he'd wondered what it would take to make her have fun, take that tired look off her face, make those blue eyes light up with laughter.

He'd also wondered what it would take to make those blue eyes light up with lust, how her face would look softened with desire. His blood began to thunder in his veins even as he shook the thought from his mind. Hands off, remember? Not his type—and he most definitely wasn't hers.

'Don't you think that maybe you expect too much from yourself? Life isn't about working from the moment you get up. It's not just the achievements that count…'

'It's not just about partying either. Not everyone has a title and a trust fund. Not everyone values those. There's more to life than casinos and boats and selfies, Leo. I couldn't bear to live such a shallow existence.'

As soon as she said the words Anna wanted to recall them. After all, Leo had given up a week to help her, had shown no sign of being the playboy the papers made him out to be. And even if he was, her anger wasn't with him, it was with her sister for blithely walking away, her mother for expecting her to take up the reins once more, with her father who sat at home, so wrapped up in *his* life he barely noticed what she had given up—what she had lost. With herself for allowing herself to be cast as the sensible, reliable one again and again. But she knew all too well what happened if she didn't step up—everything crumbled.

'I'm sorry,' she said.

Leo sat back and raised his hands in mock surrender. 'No need to apologise, Dr Gray.'

'It's just so hard to know what the right thing to do is. I mean, should I leave Dad alone to take his pills or not, like Rosa would say? Or leave Mama to flounder here alone?' Anna twisted her fingers together. 'They say opposites attract, but what no one mentions is what happens afterwards. What it's like living in a house where two people are so incompatible. My father likes everything in its place, he likes rules and routines and plans.'

'And notebooks?' Leo cast a meaningful glance at Anna's current notebook placed, as ever, within easy reach.

'And notebooks,' she agreed, unable not to answer his knowing smile with one of her own. 'Whereas Mama, well, you've met Sancia…'

He nodded, amusement dancing in his dark eyes. Anna didn't want to notice how good it felt when all his attention was on her, that direct gaze filled with warm approbation and something else, something hotter. Something that made her want to sit up, wish her hair weren't messily tied back, wish that she were wearing something other than a paint-splattered T-shirt and cut-off old shorts.

'I'd have thought that the law of averages should have meant that Rosa and I would have ended up somewhere in the middle,' Anna continued, reaching for the beer and taking a sip of the light, slightly bitter liquid. 'But although neither of us are quite as extreme, we definitely ended up on one side or the other.' She glanced back across, her whole body tingling as she saw he was still looking at her with the same unnerving intensity. Laughing a little nervously, she ducked her head down to avoid meeting his gaze head-on. 'Anyway, that's ancient history.'

But she could still feel his gaze burning into her, hotter than the afternoon sun. 'Let me get this straight. So you have no Sancia in you at all?'

'Not a drop.'

'You're never spontaneous?'

'Never. At least,' she amended, as thoughts of her student folly, her intense crush on Sebastian, and the nearly catastrophic consequences flashed through her mind, leaving a wave of hot shame in its wake, 'I have been, but it didn't end well.' Which was the understatement of the year.

He sat back, eyes alight with mischief. Anna tried to ignore the churn low down in her abdomen, mixed with an anticipation she didn't want to admit to. After all, there was nothing *to* anticipate.

'I'm all for making a plan every now and then, Anna.'

Her stomach tumbled as he drew out her name, his accent caressing each syllable, adding a slight stress on the first. 'Aaan-na.'

'That's good to hear.'

'But,' he continued as if she hadn't spoken, 'spontaneity is what gives life its spice, don't you agree?'

'I'm English.' No way was she going to let him see the swirl of excitement the dark caress of his voice invoked in her, let him see how the thrill of the unknown possibilities spiralled through her. *What was wrong with her?* She didn't do spontaneous, remember, especially not with playboys.

Leo raised his eyebrows. 'English. And?'

'We're not an island known for our spice,' Anna said, ruthlessly pushing away thoughts of steaming curry, fresh falafel, her favourite tapas bar. 'Nice, plain food, that's the English way. Preferably boiled.' Nothing like a stereotype to win an argument.

'Ah, but you're half Spanish,' Leo reminded her. 'Heat runs through your veins no matter how much you may try to dampen it.'

He spoke truer than he could have known. Heat did flare up at his words, flickering through her veins and along her arteries as if he had lit a fuse. Anna swallowed, dragging her eyes away from Leo's hypnotic gaze, down the contour of his throat, only to stutter to a stop as she reached the bronze breadth of his chest. Did the man never put a shirt on?

'I thought we already established that I'm a clone of my father.'

His voice dropped, low and suggestive. 'I don't believe that, Anna. And I don't think you do either.'

Where was the quick response, her smart put-down? She'd belonged to a debating team throughout university, for goodness' sake, she ate overconfident undergraduates for breakfast and *still* had space for elevenses, but for once Anna was utterly lost for words. Lost and floundering. She was hyper-aware of her surroundings, of the sun beating down relentlessly, the tart scent of lemons, the tang of salt drifting in on the sea breeze. Hyper-aware of colour; of the gleaming white of the freshly painted bungalow, the faded green of the shutters and low tiled roof, such a contrast to the lush greens of the overgrown trees and bushes surrounding her, the clear turquoise of the sea, fringed by the creamy yellow crescent of sand.

And overpowering it all she was hyper-aware of Leo di Marquez. Sitting almost insolently as he lounged on his chair, muscles gleaming under the sun's caress, his eyes laughing, promising something she didn't want to comprehend. Anna had felt a connection to him the day they met, unwanted, unlooked for, unknown—that was why she kept her distance. But like a greedy child she had allowed her curiosity to lead her into the gingerbread house and now she was trapped.

'Don't you think it's fun to be just a little spontaneous every now and then?' Leo continued, his voice still low, still mesmerising.

No, Anna's mind said firmly, but her mouth didn't get the memo. 'What do you have in mind?'

His mouth curved triumphantly and Anna's breath caught, her mind running with infinite possibilities, her pulse hammering, so loud she could hardly hear him for the rush of blood in her ears.

'Nothing too scary,' he said, his words far more reassuring than his tone. 'What do you say to a well-earned and unscheduled break?'

'We're having a break.'

'A proper break. Let's take out the *La Reina Pirata*—' his voice caressed his boat's name lovingly '—and see where we end up. An afternoon, an evening, out on the waves. What do you say?'

Anna reached for her notebook, as if it were a shield against his siren's song. 'There's too much to do…'

'I'm ahead of schedule.'

'We can't just head out with no destination!'

'This coastline is perfectly safe if you know

what you're doing.' He grinned wolfishly. 'I know exactly what I'm doing.'

Anna's stomach lurched even as her whole body tingled. She didn't doubt it. 'I...' She couldn't, she shouldn't, she had responsibilities, remember? Lists, more lists, and spreadsheets and budgets, all needing attention.

But Rosa would. Without a backwards glance. She wouldn't even bring a toothbrush.

Remember what happened last time you decided to act like Rosa, her conscience admonished her, but Anna didn't want to remember. Besides, this was different. She wasn't trying to impress anyone; she wasn't ridiculously besotted, she was just an overworked, overtired young woman who wanted to feel, to be, her age for a short while.

'Okay, then,' she said, rising to her feet, enjoying the surprise flaring in Leo di Marquez's far too dark, far too melting eyes. 'Let's go.'

CHAPTER FIVE

WHAT WAS SHE DOING?

Anna tried to quell the rising panic as Leo helped her into the dinghy and pushed off the jetty, rowing in sure, strong strokes towards his boat, moored just fifty yards away at the mouth of the island's tiny natural harbour. She didn't do spontaneous and she certainly didn't do spontaneous with an insanely handsome man who seemed to have a hard time locating a shirt and convincing it to stay on his impressively toned body. Although, it was hard to be too irritated by the lack of shirt when rowing showcased just how effective said muscles were, obviously both use *and* ornament.

Looking up, Anna caught Leo's eye and her cheeks burst into flame at his knowing look. She tore her gaze away and stared fixedly at the white crests of the small rippling waves, ignoring his snort of laughter.

It only took a few minutes to reach the side of *La Reina Pirata*, Leo throwing a rope to moor the dinghy alongside with practised ease. 'After you,' he said, gesturing at the narrow ladder on the side of the boat.

It wasn't easy to be graceful scrambling up a ladder that was more footholds than treads. Of course Leo bounded up after her with a careless ease born of practice and a natural athleticism. 'Welcome aboard.'

'Thank you.' But all she could do was gaze around, aware her mouth was hanging open in awe. 'This is quite something.'

The deck was ridged teak, gleaming as if freshly oiled, and ran from the cockpit, through the glass enclosed galley and the open-air seating area to the open deck at the back of the boat. Inside the galley wide padded bench seats surrounded a dining table, a state-of-the-art television and sound system dominated the other side of the cabin, and next to that a small but perfectly formed kitchen. A hatch was open, steps leading down into the interior of the boat.

'Drink?' Leo strolled over to the full-sized fridge. 'I have wine, beer, *cava*?'

'Water please,' Anna said hastily. The boat was already going to her head; the last thing she needed was alcohol discombobulating her further.

Leo handed her a glass filled with ice, fresh fruit garnishing the drink. Even the drinks were fancy on this boat. 'I'm just going to stow the dinghy. Have a look around, make yourself at home.'

Leo kept the boat suitably shipshape, not an item out of place, everything gleaming as if it had been recently waxed or polished and yet there was nobody else on board. Not what she would have expected of a careless playboy at all. His toys might be of the very best quality, but at least he looked after them.

The almost clinical tidiness continued as she made her way down to the lower deck. She'd expected it to be dark and a little claustrophobic but the glass-sided walls were tinted so that although outsiders couldn't see into the cabins, the sunlight flooded through. There were three rooms, a master suite with a perfectly made king-size bed, a second double bedroom and a study equipped with a desk and not one, but three computers, a satellite phone and a printer. 'Curiouser and curiouser,' she murmured as she scanned the room. Why on earth did Leo need so many computers?

The sound of the engines starting stopped her in her tracks. She was really doing this. Going for a trip with no planning, no foresight, nothing on her except the clothes she stood in—the dirty, paint-splattered clothes which, she was uneasily aware, made her the grubbiest thing on the boat.

She paused, fear thundering through her veins, the urge to yell out and tell Leo to stop almost overwhelming. Anna took a deep breath, and then another. Life as she knew it wasn't working; nothing was how she had thought it would be. Order and sense weren't bringing her the contentment they usually did. Taking one day—one afternoon—out to try a different path wasn't going to hurt her. And that was all this was. One afternoon. Tomorrow she would get out her lists and be Dr Anna Gray once more.

As soon as Anna reappeared on deck Leo knew something about her was different. It wasn't just that she had loosened her dark mane from its clasp, nor that she had removed her T-shirt to expose a remarkably pretty red bikini top. It was more the way her whole being seemed more relaxed, the pinched look wiped off her face, the habitual worry gone from her eyes. This was exactly what he had intended; he just hadn't expected the transformation to be so quick. Or for every atom in his body to stand up and take notice. *Easy, she's just a girl in a bikini. You've seen many girls in skimpier bikinis than that.*

But none that looked quite as sensational as Anna.

She wandered over to stand next to him, staring at the dashboard with wide eyes. 'Can I do anything?'

'Have you ever driven a boat? No? Come here, then. This is the steering wheel…'

'I have worked that one out,' she said drily.

'And this is the throttle here, and here is the gear control. Okay…' He continued to talk her through how to speed the boat up, how to slow down, brake and steer the powerful vessel, enjoying standing behind her, one arm loosely around her as he guided her hand on the throttle. The warmth of her burned into him, the subtle floral scent of her hair filling his senses. 'That's good,' he said, swallowing, aware just what an effect her proximity was having on him. 'Keep her going exactly like that.'

Stepping away was both an exquisite relief and an even more exquisite torture. He wanted to keep that arm around her, to touch the smooth skin on her back, exposed now to his gaze, only the thin red strings of her bikini contrasting with her olive skin. Her waist dipped in then flared out at the denim waistband of her shorts. Was she wearing matching bikini bottoms? *No*, he reminded himself. This afternoon might be about having fun, but it wasn't about having *that* sort of fun.

Leo swallowed. He knew there were several good reasons why, right now, he was struggling to remember them. He took another step back.

'This is great,' Anna called out, her face intent as she steered the boat through the sea. 'Where am I going?'

'Wherever you want. We can't get lost, not around here, and the tank's full.'

'Seriously? Just head off with no destination in mind?'

'Anna, that's half the fun.' It almost physically hurt as he backed further away, her scent continuing to tease his senses. He could still feel the imprint of her body against his. Leo swallowed hard, curling his hands into fists to stop himself reaching back out to her. He didn't remember ever wanting to touch someone quite so badly before.

'Just keep going, yell if you get bored. I'm off for a siesta.' He stepped back again and then again, turning to make his way out of the galley to the padded upper deck, aware of the puzzled, slightly hurt look Anna gave him as he retreated. Suddenly this trip didn't seem like the best idea he'd ever had. In fact it felt downright foolish, the two of them cooped up on a boat that usually felt so spacious, but right now seemed cramped, claustrophobic even, although he was breathing in the salt-tanged sea breeze, nothing overhead apart from blue sky and hot afternoon sun. What was going on?

Leo took a deep breath. *Let's be rational here.* He was attracted to Anna, good old plain and simple lust. It just seemed odd because he was usually careful not to get close to people of substance, of intellect. Didn't allow himself to forge ties that might have any durability. He didn't know how to handle a woman who made him sit up and think, who made him want to challenge not just who he allowed himself to be seen as, but who he truly was.

He grabbed a pair of sunglasses before lying down on the comfortable padded sun deck, folding his hands under his head and staring up at the sky. This ennui wasn't new, but it was getting more and more pervasive. It had followed him around for the last few years, tainting every success, cheering the occasional failures. After twelve years his nomadic life seemed hollow, meaningless, making money no longer gave him the same thrill—but he knew no other way.

Somehow this last week, painstakingly painting and repairing, was the most satisfying week he could remember in a long time.

Leo shifted uncomfortably. The ennui might not be new, but it had certainly intensified ever since Valentina had announced her engagement. Like him she was very careful about what she revealed to the public gaze, like him she was all myth and mystery masquerading as reality.

She didn't create, she didn't sing or act or dance, her fame solely concentrated in what she wore, where she was photographed and with whom, and she elevated what could be seen as vacuous existence to an art form. Not that he judged her, no, his little sister who had grown up knowing only poverty and deprivation deserved every moment of her success. But she *had* changed over the last year, both sharpened and softened by love. She was canny enough to use her wedding and her fiancé's connections to promote her own career, to turn herself into a serious supermodel, push her brand upmarket, but she truly loved Todd. She had lowered her defences where he was concerned, had allowed him to see the sweet young woman behind the polished, posed exterior. What had that cost her?

He'd never know, because he would never make himself so vulnerable. What if he allowed someone in and they saw that he was exactly who he thought he might be: a sharp-minded, money-making machine with no real soul? All Leo knew was that he didn't want to find out—and whether that was self-preservation or fear he had no idea. No idea at all.

He sat back up, impatient with the dark thoughts clouding what was supposed to be a carefree afternoon. He didn't do introspection, remember? He did what he pleased. And right now what he wanted was to cool off, to slew the self-doubt right off.

Anna had kept the boat going in a fairly straight trajectory, the coastline visible on the far horizon. Leo scanned it. There. Perfect. Jumping to his feet, he sauntered back to the cockpit, careful to keep his face as insouciant as possible, to ensure none of his indecision was written anywhere on his body. 'How's it going?'

'Good, as long as I don't need to change direction or speed and nothing gets in my way.' Anna turned and smiled and Leo's heart stuttered to a stop for one long moment as he drank her in, the tousled waves falling over her shoulders, the bikini revealing more than it concealed and the new, relaxed glint in her eye, the natural smile, the confidence in the way she stood. Funny, he had spent the last few moments questioning who and what he was, whereas Anna seemed to have slewed off her uptight and organised persona with the casting off of the boat.

He stood a good foot away, not sure he wanted to be within touching—or smelling—distance of Anna, not until he felt a lot more like himself. 'Fancy a swim?'

'Here?'

'Close. There's a bay just ahead. We can anchor at the mouth to it and swim off the boat.'

'Won't the water be cold?' she said, screwing her face up doubtfully. 'It's still early in the season.'

'We'll find out when we get in. Where's your sense of adventure, Dr Gray?' he added and saw the doubt clear off her face as if it had never been.

'If I get frostbite I'm suing you,' she said. 'Okay, Captain, guide me in.'

Leo took a deep breath. It would be all too easy to walk over and help her steer into the harbour, to lean against her, to put his hands against hers, to feel the suppleness of her waist, to inhale her scent, but that kind of thinking was why he needed this cold swim in the first place. It was all his own fault. He'd wanted to see Dr Gray unbuttoned—he just wasn't expecting her bikini top to show off quite so many enticing curves when she did so.

'Okay.' He leaned against the window, arms firmly folded, not allowing himself to step within touching distance. 'You need to relax your grip on the throttle and turn the wheel like that, yes, that's good, a little gentler. Keep her on that course…'

It didn't take long for Anna to steer the boat into the mouth of the cove. It was deserted, the turquoise sea lapping against the volcanic rocky shore, the cliffs rising up ensuring that the only people to enter the cove would be doing so via the sea. 'What a gorgeous spot.' Anna stood, staring out at the view, spellbound.

'I'm going to anchor the boat. It's calm today, but we still don't want it to drift off and leave us marooned here.' Although there would be worse people to be marooned on a desert island with. She would be bound to come up with a plan for food, shelter and rescue within twenty minutes of a shipwreck.

Anna followed him out onto the deck and watched as he unwound the sea anchor, casting it out, calculating just how much chain it needed this close to shore. 'Do you live on this boat all the time?' she asked as he straightened.

'Not continuously. I have an apartment in Barcelona, but I do spend most of my time on here.'

'Doesn't it get scary? Alone at sea at night?'

'I'm not often alone,' he said deliberately and watched her cheeks flush. Leo didn't want to analyse just why he was pushing his playboy credentials so hard when the truth was he hadn't actually slept with a woman in over a year. 'Nor do I moor out at sea. It can be dangerous, even with warning lights on. I'm usually in a harbour somewhere.'

'It doesn't get claustrophobic? Living in such a small place?'

'She's bigger than an average studio apartment in London or New York. Besides, who can get claustrophobic with the sky overhead, the sea all around and the knowledge that as soon as the scenery palls I can pull anchor and go wherever I wish? Cannes, Monte Carlo, Ibiza…'

'Anywhere as long as it has a coastline,' Anna pointed out.

'Anywhere I want to go does have a coastline.' Leo peered over the side of the boat, one hand on the anchor cable checking for stability. 'This looks fine. Okay, Dr Gray, let's see just how spontaneous you can be.' He flashed a smile at her as he shucked off his shorts, turned and jumped off the boat, gasping as he dived cleanly into the sharp cold.

Anna stood by the rail, laughing as Leo surfaced spluttering. 'Is the temperature good for you?' she called.

'It's perfect, come in and try it,' he called back, flipping on his front to shoot through the water with bold strong strokes. Anna couldn't stop her gaze lingering on his dark, muscled limbs, on his clean lines, the moment he had stood in front of her bare except for his swim shorts emblazoned clearly on her mind. He looked good for someone who apparently spent his life at parties, and it wasn't as if there were a gym on-board.

Strange he actually lived on a boat, even a boat as luxurious and spacious as this. It didn't look like a home; there were no photographs, no knick-knacks, nothing to personalise it at all.

Leaning over the rail, Anna looked down at the dazzling blue sea, aware how deceptive its welcoming was. Even paddling was cold; here in deeper water the temperature would be decidedly chilly. Still, she was supposed to be spontaneous, wasn't she? Remembering that she was on holiday as well as working. Rosa would already be in the water, swimming after Leo, flirtatiously instigating a water fight. In fact, she probably would just jump straight in either with her clothes on or with no clothes at all. At least Anna was wearing a bikini...

It would be spontaneous if she weren't...

A smile curved her mouth as she pictured the shock on Leo's face, the way his brown eyes would darken to black. She'd been so aware of him as he had showed her how to drive the boat, so very close she could have leaned back just a little and pressed against him. He'd been aware of her too, she knew it. If she dived in next to him, in her bikini or out of it, would that awareness be sharpened, heightened? Probably.

Did she want that? Could she handle it?

Anna shivered, her skin goosebumping despite the heat in the late spring air. What was she doing? Leo was flirty, sure, but he probably flirted more with Sancia, with Maria the maid, than he did with Anna. They had barely spoken over the last week.

Barely spoken maybe, but she had been aware of his every move, every look. And she knew he had been equally aware of her.

She should stop thinking and start doing. Have some fun for the first time in a long, long time.

And with that thought memories hit. Another swim, another man. An outdoor swimming pool, a glass of champagne or two. Memories of clothes discarded recklessly, of the way she had dived in, turning to smile provocatively, knowing he would follow. Knowing, wanting, welcoming what would happen next.

Only she hadn't been in any way prepared for what happened next. It turned out that spontaneity had consequences, that a playboy couldn't be reformed.

Almost without intending to Anna folded her arms around herself, as if she could cocoon the hurt, the memories safely inside, almost shaking with grief, with embarrassment for the naïve girl she had once been. Her hand slipped down to her stomach, pressing hard against the flatness as if she could keep all the hurt, the memories contained within. But she would never forget the scorn in Sebastian's eyes the moment before he turned and walked away from her.

Anna swallowed, her throat thick with tears. Spontaneity wasn't for her, she knew that all too well, and playboys who lived on boats were definitely not for her. Let Leo have his swim. Then she would demand he turn the boat around and take her back to La Isla Marina, back to safety and sense. Where she belonged.

CHAPTER SIX

BY THE TIME Leo finished his swim Anna had composed herself, sitting at the galley table, a glass of water before her, scrolling through her phone, barely looking up as he strode in, a towel around his shoulders, drops falling from the sleek dark head.

'You didn't want a swim?'

'Not really.' She couldn't look directly at him in case he saw through her casual tone. 'Leo, this is lovely, but…'

'You want to go back?'

'Yes, I think that's best.' She raised her eyes to his face then, but his expression was utterly inscrutable.

'Before or after dinner? Only if I remember rightly there's a great seafood restaurant along this coast, not too far along. Shame not to try it.'

Home, now, her instincts screamed, but her

good manners won out. 'Dinner would be nice. Thank you.'

Anna returned her attention to her phone, glad of the ever-present excuse of emails to occupy her, to stop her watching Leo towel himself dry. Her agent and editor had both sent impatient if encouraging questions about her progress, her father had sent a brief, terse message asking what the password was for their online supermarket account and, in the space of just a few hours, her mother had managed to send her several emails, complete with many exclamations and emojis denoting goodness knew what, Anna certainly didn't.

She reread the first of her mother's lengthy missives and couldn't help exclaiming, 'Oh, brilliant!'

Leo paused. Anna did her best not to notice how the white towel set off his tan, how the casual way it was draped over his shoulder emphasised every sculpted muscle. 'What is?'

With an effort she tore her gaze back to her phone. 'Sancia's received a huge delivery, all the wedding decorations including fairy lights, tablecloths, candles—everything we need apart from the flowers, which are apparently coming on the actual wedding day. Valentina has sent everything labelled and ready to go. That's a huge amount of work saved.'

'Val mentioned it was on its way. That reminds me, she was hoping that her favourite restaurant in Barcelona will be able to cater the actual reception. Will that cause any problems?'

'Actually it's a relief. The kitchen staff can concentrate on producing the food for the rest of the week. I know the day after the wedding Valentina wants paella on the beach, but they still have five more dinners to plan, plus all the breakfasts, lunches and snacks. Every dish has to be traditionally Spanish with vegetarian, vegan, nut-free, dairy-free and gluten-free options as well—which does make the traditionally Spanish part a little tricky.'

'I'm surprised that's all the options she's asked for. You wait till you meet her guests—and start meeting their demands. You will be earning every cent, believe me,' Leo said darkly.

Anna pushed her hair out of her eyes as she leaned back against the comfortably padded bench. 'I can't help wondering why the short notice for the wedding—and why hold it somewhere she hasn't even seen? It seems odd for someone whose life is so public to be so hands-off with something so important—my most down-to-earth friends are completely consumed by their weddings. I can't imagine any of them getting married somewhere they haven't actually been to!'

She still wasn't sure why Leo was here on Valentina's behalf. He obviously cared enough about her to consider her to be like a sister to him, but apart from their nationality they appeared to have nothing in common. Valentina lived in New York, was an Internet princess and hung out with a group of privileged, beautiful, fashionistas; Leo lived in Spain and his social group, although equally privileged, was much wilder. And nothing Anna had come across on social media linked them in any way. Not one photograph, not one friend in common, nothing except they were both Spanish, both hailed from near Barcelona.

'La Isla Marina wasn't the original venue,' Leo said, pulling on a T-shirt, to Anna's equal relief and disappointment, before he slid onto the opposite bench, grabbing her glass of water and taking a long sip. 'She was planning to hold the wedding at the villa in Ibiza where she met Todd.'

It all began to make a little more sense. 'What happened?'

'Fire, catastrophic apparently. There was no way the villa could be repaired in time. She needed somewhere here, in Spain, able to host one hundred and fifty guests for the week on just over a month's notice...'

'Where better than a resort so down on its luck, they had no guests for the start of the season at all? Lucky for her, lucky for Mama. But she knows nothing about us *or* La Isla Marina. I know she's busy, but I can't believe she hasn't visited yet to check everything out.'

'She spent several summers on the island when she was a child. She has very fond memories of it. That's why she was so keen to relocate the wedding to it. Why I'm so keen to make sure it's ready for her.'

'She was a guest on La Isla Marina? When?' Not recently, obviously, but if Valentina had spent a holiday when the island was in its heyday then it was no wonder she had switched the wedding over; when it was at its best there was nowhere more magical. More romantic.

Leo shook his head. 'Not a guest. Her mother worked for your grandparents for two or three summers starting when Valentina was around eight. That's why she knows it so well. She lived there too over those summers.'

Anna thought back, but there was no niggle of recognition. Her grandparents had often hired couples as seasonal workers and as a result there had usually been a small gaggle of workers' children running around the place. Families were housed in small apartments in and around the villa, the children looked after at the same holiday clubs as those set up for island guests. 'When she was eight? She's what? Twenty-one now? That means she would have been there when we still went for the whole summer. Only I doubt I would have taken much notice of her,' she added.

'*Sí*, I'm sure a maid's daughter was far too below the owners' granddaughter to be noticed.' His voice was cutting.

'No.' She sat up, indignation crashing through

her at Leo's scathing tone, her face hot. 'Not at all, but if she was eight I was fifteen and at that age that's an entire generation gap. The different ages didn't mix, but that was the only barrier. Some of my best summer friends had parents who worked on La Isla Marina, only a few were visitors. That was really uncalled for.'

'I apologise. It's just people can be...' he paused '...rigid, about things like class.'

'Well, I'm not and nor were my grandparents. Mama will remember her, I'm sure. So the wedding is a homecoming?' That made a difference, somehow. Welcome as the money would be to Sancia, making this effort for one of the island's daughters seemed right somehow.

'A homecoming?' he echoed. 'Maybe it is. Lucky Valentina, to have a place she considers home.' He slid out of his seat, his face shuttered. 'I'll go and haul in the anchor. Let me know if you want to try that restaurant or head straight back. I don't mind either way.'

With a deep sigh Anna slumped onto the table. Even though her aim had been to put the brakes on whatever might or might not be simmering between Leo and her, she still couldn't help feeling that she'd blown it. Not just ending the new accord between them, but reverting to type. Sensible Anna didn't sail away with handsome pirates, sensible Anna didn't leave chores undone, sensible Anna didn't swim in cold seas. Sensible Anna didn't get hurt; she didn't have much fun either, but that was the trade-off she made. That was what kept her safe.

Somehow the knowledge didn't give her the same satisfaction it usually did. Safe was a book unwritten, a father who couldn't even order his own shopping, a mother content to leave Anna to sort out her problems for her, a sister she didn't see or speak to. A sister who would never waste an afternoon on a boat with a handsome man checking emails and worrying about the future.

What would it be like when Rosa finally turned up? Anna could already see the amused scorn in Rosa's face, how she would love the knowledge that Anna had spent so much time with a gorgeous, occasionally charming man and spent it doing chores. How satisfying would it be if she and Leo were on friendly terms when Rosa did deign to rock up?

By the time they got back the light would be

almost gone; they wouldn't be able to do any more work today. So why not extend the trip for a few hours? Continue with careful spontaneity. Yes to a sail and a meal, both civilised activities. No to the intimacy of swimming, no to reacting to his every light touch, no to lingering glances.

Just because Leo discombobulated Anna, just because he made her want things she knew weren't good for her to want, made her feel fusty and stuffy and dull, just because every quirk of his mouth dared her to take risks she had no intention of taking didn't mean they couldn't be friends.

Besides, it still stung that he thought she was the kind of person who would stand on her dignity, that she would consider a maid's daughter her inferior. What they needed was a new start. She would be her most charming through dinner and Leo di Marquez y Correa would have no choice but to see that there was more to her than notebooks and efficiency.

Pushing back his chair, Leo stretched and glanced at his watch. Two hours had disappeared in a flow of emails and reports and he had barely made a dent. Over the last week he'd neglected his business and his out-of-control inbox reflected it. There were still far too many decisions to be made, reports to be read, to be commissioned, to be acted upon. Funny to think he'd once got such a thrill from moving such huge sums of money around, from creating wealth, bestowing it. Now it just seemed nebulous, more like playing a video game than work. Not like painting and repairing. Maybe he should give it all up and become a full-time groundskeeper? He smiled wryly. Would his father consider that a step up or a step down from a professional playboy and gambler? He suspected a step down.

He glanced at his watch again; another hour until the restaurant opened. They'd moored at the little seashore village's small wooden harbour earlier that afternoon, but Anna had turned down Leo's offer of a walk, preferring her emails and making even more of her interminable lists. She'd erected another layer of protection around herself while he swam, the laughing girl who'd driven his boat once more replaced with the cool, organised woman with a large *keep out* sign stapled to her forehead.

A sign he had every intention of respecting.

'Leo, I've just realised all I have is what I'm standing up in…oh, I'm sorry, I didn't realise you were busy. I didn't mean to disturb you.' Leo was so engrossed in his thoughts he didn't hear the door open. Anna peered around it, staring at his three computer screens with unabashed curiosity. 'What on earth are you doing?'

She stepped into the room, still transfixed by the screens. Leo shot them a brief glance, checking nothing incriminating or confidential was on display; one showed the day's open stock markets, another the report he was currently working on, the third his emails. Innocuous if peculiar for a man who supposedly did nothing but cruise the seas and party. *'Nada importante,'* he said quickly.

'No? It looks important. You were a hundred miles away. You didn't even hear me call you.' She stepped closer. 'I wondered why you had three computers in here.'

Turning on his best lazy smile, Leo moved slightly, blocking his email. 'It's important to know what's going on when sailing. I'm just checking the weather forecast.'

The lift of her eyebrows showed just how far short he was of convincing her. 'Funny, that looks far more like the FTSE than the Met to me.'

He turned up the wattage on his smile, adding a hint of roguish for good measure. 'Gambling takes more than one form, you know.'

'True, but stocks and shares are for some reason seen as a lot more respectable than the roulette wheel. Is that what you're doing? Trading? And what's that?' She nodded at the report.

Leo had hidden behind a faceless company name for so long, hidden behind a false image of a partying gambler for so long, he sometimes forgot why the charade had started. It was second instinct to keep pretending. Hiding. But the curiosity in Anna's sharp gaze tugged at him and he knew he wanted to see the change in her face when he told her exactly what he was doing, to see that faint, unconscious superiority she employed turn to respect. Hardly anyone beyond his employees, faceless anonymous employees working in virtual offices all around the globe, knew what he did. It would be nice for someone he respected to know.

'Leo?' She sounded concerned now. 'I'm sorry, am I intruding? I was only joking. It doesn't matter. My question can wait…'

'It's not the FTSE, it's the Dow Jones,' he said abruptly and watched the blue eyes widen.

'So you do gamble with stocks as well as at casinos?'

'No, I invest.'

'In shares?'

'At first, but now I invest in companies. Preferably in start-ups, although sometimes in companies who want to expand, or are in trouble and need to turn around. The term is angel, I believe. I put money in, usually with conditions, although that depends on the company, and then they pay me back with interest or I retain a share of the company.'

'But…how? Nothing I read said that you were interested in investments.'

'That's because nobody knows. It doesn't quite fit the image, does it? My company itself is the investor. I'm not publicly listed as the owner. Any investigator would have to look hard to find my connection to it—and why would they? We don't invest in controversial projects. We're an ethical investor. There's nothing to spark their interest.'

Anna's mouth was open, but no words were coming out, which, Leo suspected, was a first. She pulled out a chair and sat down heavily, staring at the rapidly changing screen displaying all the stock movements of the day. 'You are telling me that you are a playboy gambler with a secret identity? Like Batman? Do you have a cape as well? Does this boat turn into a plane?' She shook her head, her hair, once more respectably confined into a ponytail, swinging with the movement. 'I've heard of secret gamblers, but not the other way round.'

'No cape, no fighting villains, just investing. And despite the title I'm no angel. I do it all for profit.'

That wasn't entirely true, not any more. Sometimes he invested because a young company had such vision, such passion, he wanted to be part of it in some way. In the hope that passion, that belief would somehow rub off on him. He was still waiting.

Anna regarded him keenly, curiosity brightening her clear, blue eyes. 'Is this how you make a living? Not in casinos?'

'I've never gambled a penny I wasn't prepared to lose.' Leo shifted, her scrutiny making him uncomfortable. 'You had a question when you burst in here. What is it?'

'A question? Right. The trouble with spontaneity...' Anna tugged at her paint-splattered shorts and grimaced '...is the lack of planning. I have nothing suitable for a restaurant at all. I can't turn up in these and a dirty T-shirt. Maybe we should head home after all.'

'There are clothes in the spare bedroom.' He scanned her slim figure, trying not to let his gaze linger on the curve of her breasts. 'Valentina sometimes joins me here when she is in between jobs. I think you're not too dissimilar a size. Help yourself to anything. There's plenty of hot water if you want a shower.'

'Thank you.' She got to her feet, headed for the door then turned. 'Leo, why is it such a secret? Investing in start-ups is a great way to make a living. Why let the world think you're nothing but a party-going playboy when there's so much more to you?'

So much more? He might not make his living the way the world thought, but he wasn't sure that meant that he was worth anything. Anna might be intelligent, but she had missed the mark this time.

He pushed out of his chair, wanting, needing to shut the conversation down. 'Come on, I'll show you the clothes and how the shower works.'

Anna followed him out of the study, across the narrow corridor and into the guest cabin at the very front of the boat. The bed was made up. Leo tried not to look at the crisp white sheets, tried to push the thought of how Anna would look entangled in them from his mind.

He'd invited Anna for a sail on a whim, purely because he enjoyed discombobulating her. What he hadn't taken into consideration was how she might affect him. He was so used to always having the upper hand, it hadn't occurred to him that a smart, curious woman like Anna was more than capable of seeing through him, seeing into him.

She liked facts, knowledge and solving problems. She had a keen intellect. And when that scrutiny was turned on him, it was like a compulsion. He'd been more honest with Anna Gray than he had been with any other human being for a very long time, including himself.

'Wardrobe's there,' he said brusquely. 'And the shower is in here.'

Anna opened the folding doors and peered in at the tiny but tidy en-suite bathroom. 'Very nice, not that I've come to expect anything else from this boat.'

'Press that button to activate the water. You can adjust the heat and power with those handles. Towels are in the wardrobe, and I believe Valentina has left toiletries in the bathroom cabinet. You should have everything you need.' Rattling off the instructions made him feel a little like Anna must with her lists, like restoring order to a suddenly disordered world. And her world was disordered for all her calm exterior; a mother who needed her, a sister she didn't speak to. No wonder she tried to restore order wherever she saw it. As long as she didn't try to restore him…

'Thank you. This is incredible.'

'Right.' He most certainly wasn't going to hang around, to imagine Anna pulling off her shirt, untying her bikini-top strings, slipping her shorts down her strong, toned legs, stepping into that shower. *Get a grip*, Leo told himself fiercely. This enforced abstinence wasn't good for him. He needed one of his no-strings, no-effort, short-term affairs and soon. Good thing there was a wedding coming up. They were usually good for a quick, fun fling. 'I'll leave you to…'

Leo stepped back and, at the same moment, Anna stepped back, straight into him, her warm body colliding hard with his. Instinctively Leo reached out, grabbing onto her, his arms pulling her close as she struggled to regain her balance. For one long second she relaxed against him, every slim curve snuggled into him, the scent of her enfolding him even as his body enfolded her.

Lust rushed through him, hard, fast, intense and all-consuming, his blood hammering through his veins, thundering in his ears. *Want. Need. Have.* His body was issuing demands, demands he wanted more than anything to accede to and Leo's arms tightened around her body, holding her closer for one incendiary moment.

Did she feel it too? Was lust shivering through her? Were her nerves humming with desire? Were her eyes dark, her mouth dry, every atom of her attuned to his? Leo didn't know what would be worse—if she did or if she didn't. If this lust was one-sided that would be humiliating enough, but if it burnt through them both then how much worse would it be when she discovered just how hollow he was? Leo spent a great deal of time making sure no one got close enough to reject him, making sure he was the first to walk away.

Letting her go, stepping back, finding the right, unconcerned smile, felt like a Herculean task and yet somehow he did. 'Careful,' he said in a voice that didn't sound like his, aware of the slight tremor as he spoke.

Anna's eyelashes fluttered down, shielding her eyes, allowing him to think he might have imagined the flicker of hurt, of disappointment in her eyes. But her voice was completely unconcerned, as matter of fact as ever. 'If I'm this clumsy when we're moored imagine what I'd be like in the middle of the ocean. I'd say a pirate's life is not for me.'

On these last words she turned, flashed him a quick smile, and disappeared into the bathroom leaving Leo standing in the cabin. Alone. The way he chose to be. The way he preferred to be. At least, that was what he told himself. One day he might even believe it.

CHAPTER SEVEN

ANOTHER LONG SILENCE fell over the table. Anna cast around for something to say and, in desperation, fell on platitudes. 'This is beautiful!'

It was a warm night and they'd been seated on the restaurant terrace overlooking the sea. The sun had already set, leaving just a few purple and grey traces in the star-strewn sky. A soft glow fell across the terrace from the tiny lanterns hanging from the flower-twined beams that connected the terrace to the building, candles illuminating the table. Blankets hung on the backs of their chairs in case the night chilled.

'Really beautiful,' she added. Leo had been practically monosyllabic since that moment in the cabin, the moment when their bodies had collided, when he had broken her fall. She'd never felt anything like the explosive attraction, as if his light clasp on her waist had ignited a fuse burning straight through her. Neither of them had moved for a long, sizzling second, their bodies perfectly melded together, their pulses beating in perfect harmony. If she'd turned would he have kissed her? All she knew was that she would have kissed him back. Only he had let go, stepped away, and since then had kept his distance physically and emotionally. Which was for the best—hadn't she decided to go for a cordial friendship, not heat-filled passion? After all, passion never ended well for her.

She couldn't help replaying that moment over and over though, and in the replay it never ended with Leo stepping away.

No, she wasn't going to think about that now, not when they were alone on this candlelit terrace, the sea serenading them. Summoning her best bright, friendly smile, Anna looked at Leo, only to find his eyes on her, not the view. 'Yes,' he said softly. 'Very beautiful.'

Heat flushed her cheeks and she glanced down at her empty plate, wishing for food, anything to occupy her hands. Truth was she *felt* beautiful tonight. Unlike herself. Valentina had left the kind of luxurious creams and cosmetics Anna didn't usually look at, let alone buy, in the small cabin and by the time she had washed her hair and applied a little make-up she already felt like the 'after' photo in a makeover.

Choosing an outfit had been a little harder. Valentina's tastes ran to skimpy and barely there, none of which fitted the friendly and cordial brief. In the end Anna had selected a silky slip dress, pleased with the way the deep, shimmering red gave a warm glow to her skin.

'Thank you for letting me pilfer Valentina's wardrobe,' she said, pulling at the gold, filmy scarf she had flung over her almost bare shoulders with nervous fingers. 'The clothes in that small wardrobe probably cost more than everything I have ever bought added together. Are you sure Valentina won't mind me wearing this?'

'She's probably forgotten she even owns it. She never wears the same outfit twice anyway, you know.'

Anna tried to imagine discarding clothes after just one wear and failed. She still had tops she'd bought while at school. 'Never? Wow. I live in the same clothes day in, day out. I can't imagine wearing something this lovely just the once.'

'She gets paid to wear them, or sent them for

free.' Leo nodded at the menu. 'Have you decided what you would like to order?'

'I'm going to go with the fish of the day.' Anna put the simple, handwritten menu down onto the table and propped her elbows on it, resting her chin in her hands as she studied the man opposite. Today, she couldn't help feeling that she'd learned more about him than he usually let slip to anyone, but there were still unanswered questions nagging at her. And keeping up a flow of conversation would mean less time for meaningful glances, less time for traitorous thoughts. 'Leo?'

'*Sí?*'

'What are you really doing spending so much time on La Isla Marina?' She glanced down at his tanned, capable-looking hands, noting the scratch he'd received from an over-enthusiastic chisel. 'Why spend a whole month getting your hands dirty?'

'For my sister,' he said.

There was something here she simply wasn't grasping. Anna frowned. 'Did you know her when you were little? How on earth does the son of a *conde* and…?'

'The illegitimate daughter of the same *conde*.'

Of course. Now it all made sense…

'She really is your sister? I assumed it was an honorary term.'

'No, there's nothing honourable about our relationship. My father seduced her mother with lies and promises he had no intention of keeping—and then when he found out she was pregnant he sacked her. She spent her winters juggling as many jobs as she could, her summers cleaning and waitressing and counting on tips to get her through the leaner months. As soon as Valentina was old enough to help she was working too. That's why I have given up a month to give her a dream wedding. I couldn't help her then, but I can and will help her now. No matter what I have to do.'

'But, it's the twenty-first century! People have rights. Didn't he have to at least pay maintenance? She should have taken him to court or…'

Leo's smile was so cold Anna stuttered to an abrupt stop. 'Assumptia, Val's mother, was too scared to fight. You have to understand, my father is a very powerful man. No one can force him to do anything he doesn't want to do. He told her that if she chose to have the baby, it would be her problem alone. Nothing to do with him. My father always keeps his word,' he added, reaching for his glass of rioja. 'In the end Assumptia decided that, hard as things were, it would be better for her and Valentina to stay away from my father. To be free.'

Anna swallowed, memories rising for the second time that day, bitter and poignant. 'That poor woman, pregnant and alone.' She couldn't keep a melancholy knowledge from her voice and Leo looked at her sharply. She didn't return his gaze, keeping her own focussed out to sea. 'When did you find out that you had a sister? Or have you always known?'

Leo paused as the waiter came over with bread and oil and to take their orders. 'Assumptia, her mother, came to work for us when I was seven or eight. My parents were absent a lot, and even when they were home they didn't spend much time with me. The house I grew up in was very old, very large, a little frightening for a young boy with an overactive imagination. I was left alone a lot. Most of the maids didn't want to bother with a small, silent boy, but Assumptia was kind to me. I loved her very much.'

Anna's heart ached as she pictured the scene, pictured the small boy alone with no one who really cared for him. Whatever her parents' faults they had loved Anna and Rosa. True, they argued, but they did their best to provide a stable, loving home. And when Anna was small, when their marriage had worked, life had been wonderful. Even when things began to fall apart, when she had become the peacemaker, she still had had the long summers with her grandparents where she was safe and free. Leo might look as if he had everything in the world—money, looks, a title—but he had grown up with nothing. 'What happened?'

'I got back from school and she was gone.' He shrugged. 'It wasn't the first time this had happened. After a while I forgot about her. There were so many different maids, you see, although not all were…kind.' He paused before he said the word, and Anna shivered in empathy, her throat thick as she listened. 'Ten years later I was at the coast and stopped at one of the beachside bars for a drink. She brought my beer to my table and

I knew her immediately, greeted her as if she were my long-lost relation, which in a way she was.' His eyes were shadowed as he reminisced.

'Was she glad to see you?'

'No, not at first. She seemed cold, cagey, but you see…' He paused then, as if searching for the right words. 'The thing is, Anna, at that time I was used to people leaving, to being considered as little more than my name and heritage.' Anna blinked at the hollowness in his voice and realisation struck her, cold and true. Leo di Marquez y Correa still felt that way. Still assumed people were only interested in *who* he was, not what he was. Was that why he hid behind his playboy image?

'Valentina ran over and straight away I knew… The way she looked, her age. Maybe in some way I had always known. There must have been rumours and gossip at the time. Val was around ten, already helping wash dishes, collecting glasses, working while other children played on the beach. I vowed then that she would be able to play, that she would have her childhood, that I would take care of her.'

'You were eighteen,' Anna said softly. 'Not much more than a child yourself.'

'Old enough.'

She leaned forward, propping her elbows on the table, absorbed in the sad tale. 'What did you do? Did you talk to your father?'

'Despite how cold and critical he was, I thought maybe he didn't know. He always told me that to be a di Marquez was to have honour. That our family was very old, very revered, that I must never let it down.' His voice dripped bitterness and Anna shivered, reaching for her wine glass. 'I couldn't imagine that he would let a child of his wash up at a cheap bar by the shore, let a child of his go hungry. I was wrong. He told me never to mention her existence. Not to be a sentimental fool. That accidents happen, but what matters is keeping them quiet, that I'd learn that as long as I uphold the family name in public, I could do anything I liked in private, that's how it is for people like us.'

'Nice,' Anna murmured, the need to comfort him overwhelming her. She stretched a hand across the table and took his. Leo sat motionless for a second and then his strong fingers enfolded hers, as if she were a lifeline connecting him to the present.

'My eyes were opened then. The family name I had been brought up to revere was nothing but hypocrisy. My duty was to keep up appearances, to be seen to be responsible, a credit to the family, do the right degree, get the right job, marry a girl whose blood was as blue as mine, ensure there were several heirs, as soon as possible, and in return I would have money to enjoy any vice I wish as long as I was discreet. I wanted no part of it. I decided then that my vices would always be there for the world to see.'

Anna tightened her grip on his, wishing she could find that hurt, lonely boy and make it all right for him—and find his parents and tell them exactly what she thought of them. 'If we can't go crazy at eighteen, then when can we?'

Leo's eyes gleamed. 'Surely you were never crazy, not even at eighteen, Dr Gray.'

'Me?' She didn't have to think back, the past always with her. 'I fell in love, totally, wholly, lost myself in love. There's nothing crazier than that.'

A flicker of something dark passed over his

face. For a moment Anna almost thought it was jealousy, although his voice was light and teasing. 'Love doesn't sound too bad.'

'Infatuation is a disease. I lost myself entirely. It was more than bad.'

'I take it he's no longer around?'

'I haven't seen him in years.' Truth was she avoided any situation where Sebastian Montague-Hughes might be seen. Even the sight of an arrogant profile resembling his was enough to make her nauseous, her chest tight.

'Replaced him with a sensible man who ticks every box on your list?'

Anna knew exactly the kind of man she wanted to settle down with one day. Someone reliable, someone with good morals and ethics. Someone safe. Not an entitled rich boy, nor, much as her heart sped up around Leo, an aristocratic Spanish pirate with issues deeper than the seas he sailed. But not yet. 'My work is my passion now.' She paused. 'At least it was.'

'Was?'

'I've had to be very dedicated to get this far so young. I just can't help wondering if this is it, can I carry on doing the same thing for the next forty years.' Sometimes, when Anna looked into the future, she could see the walls closing in, trapping her in a world she wasn't sure was for her at all. 'You know, when Mama called and begged me to come and help out I didn't say yes because I'm the good daughter who always does what's expected. I said yes because I needed to get away from Oxford for a while. I needed some space.' She searched for a change of subject, not wanting to think any more about her dilemma. 'So, number five on *Titles* magazine's *"Wicked Aristocrats We'd Like to Redeem"* list, how is the playboy lifestyle? As much fun as you hoped it would be?'

His smile was pure wickedness. 'Care to find out?'

Luckily for Anna the waiter brought out their food before she could formulate a response that didn't involve stammering, blushing, or turning into Dr Gray with a withering put-down. The fish and perfectly grilled vegetables were delicious and, by unspoken accord, they moved on to lighter topics, discussing the plans for the week ahead, how Valentina wanted the decorations to be displayed and how she had first met Todd.

Although Anna was mostly relieved by the change in intensity, part of her was a little frustrated. She sensed that Leo rarely let anyone in, that she was in a privileged position—and that every time he did more and more of her preconceptions were chipped away.

Her preconceptions were her armour, protecting her from a man she was no way equipped to handle. Leo's arrogance, his bearing, his confidence might in turn be his armour, but they were also part of him, forged while he was young, in anger and defensiveness. He might despise his parents and all they stood for, but there was a pride in his bearing, in his manner, that was all born of an old name, old money and a sense of knowing who he was and what he stood for.

But, like the expert researcher she was, she wanted more. Now he had opened the chink she wanted to reach further inside, to expose all he was, all he felt. She'd been here before—and she'd got it so horribly wrong last time. Was she just repeating the same mistakes? She had assumed there was more to Sebastian, that he had hidden depths, depths only she could find. Assumed she could reform him with love, make him into the man she dreamed he was. She'd been brutally, horribly wrong. If she allowed herself to fall for Leo and be wrong again then it might break her.

But somehow she knew it might be far too late.

Leo was silent as he escorted Anna back to the boat. It was ironic. Just twelve hours ago he had been looking at a painted wall with complete satisfaction. Now he felt as if he'd spent an hour in the confessional, scourged and empty. Not that he'd been to confession since he'd left his parents' house. His father still went every week. Did he feel absolved of his sins? Was that why he felt able to carry on with impunity? Leo preferred to carry his with him, companions on a long, weary road.

'You might as well get some sleep as we sail back,' he said a little brusquely once they were both safely aboard. 'It will take a couple of hours to sail back to La Isla Marina at this time of night. The spare cabin is freshly made up—you can sleep there.'

'It's very late though,' Anna pointed out. 'Why don't we just stay here and sail back first thing in the morning?'

'Won't your mother worry?'

Anna held up her phone. 'I can text her. The only problem is she will never believe that we're not, you know…she'll probably hang out bunting to celebrate.'

Leo arched a brow. 'You know?'

Folding her arms, Anna threw him a scathing glare. 'You do know so don't pretend.'

He did know, and he didn't want to dwell on the thought. Not when he could imagine it so clearly, could almost taste the lushness of her mouth, feel the silk of her skin under his fingertips. But Leo wasn't his father, he only slept with women who wanted what he did—a momentary comfort.

He sought for the right tone of his voice, to keep his face relaxed even as his blood heated. 'She'll hang out bunting, not be waiting for me with a pitchfork?'

'With an entire band to welcome us back in style. My mother thinks I'm boring. You probably agree.'

Boring he could handle. Right now he was yearning for boring. 'Boring? No. Organised? Oh, yes.' He paused, knowing he should leave the conversation there, but something about the evening's frank exchanges compelled him to carry on. 'Afraid? Definitely!'

'Afraid?' Anna sounded indignant. 'Rubbish! Just look at the last two weeks. I took a month's holiday with no notice to come and help organise a wedding, despite knowing nothing about weddings. I came sailing with you on a moment's notice…'

'I take it back.' Leo held his hands up. 'You're a lioness.'

But Anna's expression clouded. 'There's nothing wrong with being careful,' she said. 'That's all I am, not afraid, careful. It's not fun having your heart broken, not fun seeing your dreams evaporate. Believe me, I've tried it.'

With a jolt Leo realised that he hadn't. He'd never fallen in love and so his heart was completely intact; he'd never had a dream worth following. He'd made money without aim or purpose, finding he was good at it. Maybe by investing in other people's dreams he tried to inhale them second-hand, but the satisfaction was as muted as the effort.

He laughed at Anna for her lists and caution, but at least she had put herself out there once. Who was the real coward here?

He pushed the unwelcome thought aside. 'So that's it, then, you tried it once, it didn't work and so now you're going to live your life according to to-do lists? No interruptions or deviations?' It seemed wrong. There was fire in Anna, he could see it, muted now, damped down, but there. Every now and then a gleam in her eye showed just how hot it could burn if she ever let go. It would be something to see if she ever did, definitely worth getting burned just to bask in her heat.

Moving over to the deck rail, Anna leaned on it, staring out at the starlit sea. 'I'm not saying I don't sometimes wish it could be different,' she said, so softly that he could only just make out her words. 'Mama and Rosa certainly seem to have more fun. Of course they do. Acting without thought, without consequences, letting someone else always pick up the pieces is by far the better way to live, if you're lucky enough to be able to.'

'Why can't you?' Leo wandered over and joined her at the rail, his hand lying next to hers.

She laughed. 'It's not in my make-up. I need facts, timetables, to explore every option, otherwise I worry and fret. But being the sensible one is exhausting.' Her voice lowered even more. 'Lonely.'

'It doesn't have to be.' Leo covered her hand with his, no idea of seduction in his mind, just the need to give comfort as she had comforted him earlier.

'I don't know any other way, not any more. I don't know *how* to take a risk, how to let anyone in. You're right, I am a coward.'

'No.' His hand tightened over hers. 'You've just left no space in your life for you, that's all. I know you spent the hour before we went out for dinner ordering groceries for your dad. Your mother has just placed every decision about getting the island ready for the season on your shoulders, even though you have a job and should have a life of your own. You need to learn to say no, Anna.'

'It's that easy?'

'Worth a shot every now and then. What would Sancia have done if you hadn't come along?'

'She'd have been all right. A handsome pirate with some keen DIY skills happened to moor up in her harbour the very next day.'

'Handsome?'

She looked up at him then, a smile finally curving her full mouth. 'Oh, as if you don't know. No one spends that much time shirtless if he doesn't know full well he has swoonworthy abs.'

Leo's heart slowed, every nerve centred on the palm of his hand, on the warmth of Anna's slightly roughened hand under his, the delicacy of her bones. 'You know, I think I've told you more of my secrets in one day than I've ever told anyone else. That makes you a very dangerous woman, Dr Gray.'

'Me?'

'You,' he confirmed. Was it his imagination, or was the space between them shrinking? He couldn't see, wasn't aware of anything but Anna, the touch of her hand in his, those luminous eyes fixed so intensely on his. She'd dropped the scarf once they'd got aboard, her shoulders now almost bare except for the merest sliver of red silk, the dress caressing her like a second skin, swaying with every movement, emphasising the curve of her waist, the length of her legs, the swell of her breasts. He swallowed. 'It's most unfair,' he said hoarsely.

'Are you scared?'

The space had definitely shrunk down to just her, moon-bright under the midnight sky.

'Scared?'

'I am,' she whispered. 'Scared that I won't live with myself if I kiss you. More scared that I won't live with myself if I don't.'

'Anna.' He couldn't believe he was about to say this, that he wasn't tasting her, touching her right now. 'I don't do relationships. I might not be the party-going playboy the world thinks I am, but I'm a strictly no-strings man. Save your kisses for someone who deserves them.'

'Leo, relax. I'm not asking for an engagement ring. I'm not even asking for a date. I just want to be someone different for one night. No to-do lists, no plans.' She bit her lip, her cheeks flushed. 'I mean, obviously there's a few things we'd need to think about. Ground rules, contraception…'

'I thought,' Leo said slowly, trying to rein in the blood thundering around his body, to silence the voice in his head yelling at him to just kiss her already, 'you were talking about a kiss…'

The flush heightened. 'As a universally agreed starting-off point, but I'd be willing to see where it led. It's never too early to talk about contraception. We're both adults, aren't we?'

Dios mio. Did she have any idea what she was saying? Leo tried desperately to recall all the reasons he needed to stay away, but they had slipped beyond his reach. 'Anna.' It was a question and an entreaty all bound up in her name.

'I know what I'm doing. Do you want me, Leo?'

'I don't think there's a man alive who wouldn't want you tonight, Anna.'

'Then stop over-thinking. That's my role.'

Leo stood, fighting for control. He'd promised himself that Anna was safe with him—he hadn't expected her to be so upfront, so unafraid. 'You're sure?'

Her fingers curled around his as she nodded,

and then his mouth was finally on hers, sweet, a little uncertain as she stood rigid for the first second until, with a small gasp, she yielded against him, her body pliant, moulding into his as the kiss intensified. Freed by her response, Leo crushed Anna closer, one hand sliding through her thick wavy hair, the other slipping around her waist. It was as if she was made to kiss him, every inch of her fitting him exactly, the softness of her breasts against his chest, her leg winding around his as she pressed ever closer.

He'd never been so stirred by a simple kiss, never been brought down by the merest touch, never been so undone by a woman's response. Leo didn't have a home, but somehow he knew that kissing Anna was the closest he would get. In a dim recess of his mind he knew that he needed to put a stop to this now, that he needed to walk away. But it was too late. He was lost.

She tasted like the sea breeze on a summer's night, like a citrus grove, like the best vintage wine, heading straight to his brain until Leo was consumed by her. His hands moved to her shoulders, caressing the silk of her bare flesh until he found those thin, tiny straps and pushed them down, over her shoulders. He wanted no barriers between them, nothing but flesh and touch, kisses and need, and, judging by the way Anna was impatiently working his buttons, she felt the same way. 'Got it,' she murmured against his mouth as she finally managed the last button, pushing his shirt off his shoulders with a ruthless abandon he could only admire.

Pausing, Leo caught her wrists as they moved with exquisite torture down his chest, his abdomen, towards his waistband. 'Anna, is this really what you want?'

She was panting as she pulled her wrists free. 'You said yourself I'm dangerous, Leo. If I was you I'd stop talking and help me get this dress off.'

And he could only oblige.

CHAPTER EIGHT

'MORNING, SLEEPYHEAD.'

Leo sounded disgustingly chirpy as Anna walked into the gallery. How did he manage that when she knew, to the second, just how little sleep he had had?

'Your English is very good. How do you know so much slang?' she said as she headed straight to the coffee machine, trying not to touch her swollen mouth, to ignore the faint soreness between her thighs, feeling as if both were lit up in neon, signalling exactly what she had got up to last night.

'English nannies, only the best for the son of the Conde de Olvares. I was brought up to have tea and supper, and to spend far too much time going on afternoon walks.'

'Poor Little Boy Fauntleroy,' Anna hadn't been entirely sure how to greet Leo, but now she was right next to him it seemed silly not to kiss his cheek, a kiss that all too easily slid to his mouth. 'Morning,' she added breathlessly.

'You look good in my shirts,' Leo said, looking at her with an undisguised approval, which heated Anna more than the coffee.

'You see, that's because I do this radical thing where I button shirts up,' she said, trying not to stare too hard at Leo's only half-covered chest and remember just how every part of that chest had tasted. 'How long have you been up?'

'An hour or so. We're only about twenty minutes away now,' he said and Anna instantly sobered up. The island, jobs, responsibilities, real life. She didn't regret for a second her boldness of the night before; she just wasn't sure how to act here in the morning after. It wasn't as if she had much practice. At least this time she had been sensible enough to talk about protection early—to control the spontaneity, to put sensible limits on the recklessness. 'Look, Leo, I'm not the kind of girl who usually has one-night stands,' she said, needing to keep some kind of control over the situation.

'Me neither,' he said to her surprise. 'I'm more

of a "let's see where this goes until one of us gets bored" kind of guy.'

Anna narrowed her eyes. 'And do you usually get bored first? Quickly?'

'*Sí.*' She was sure he had practised that boyish grin in front of the mirror; it was far too disarming. 'Always. But then I have never had an opponent as dangerous as you before.'

'So what do we do, just pretend last night didn't happen?'

'Now that,' he said softly, eyes locked on hers, 'would be a shame. I suggest we try it my way. Have fun until one of us gets bored.'

'Such a smooth talker,' Anna said, but her heart was racing at the prospect of three more weeks with Leo. Three weeks with a man who challenged her, laughed at her, made her laugh at herself. It was probably exactly what she needed. Time out of her usual life, new experiences, new perspectives. 'But there is some logic in what you say, looked at objectively, I mean.'

'There is?'

'Well, we are kind of stuck with each other.'

'True.' The gleam in his dark eyes made her

heart beat faster. She swallowed, aiming for cool and collected.

'Besides, I suppose last night wasn't too bad.'

'Ah,' he murmured. 'The English gift of understatement.'

The gleam intensified and her knees buckled at the suggestion in them. Not too bad wasn't just an understatement; it verged on slander.

'And everyone needs a hobby.'

'Anna.' He drew out the syllables of her name in the way guaranteed to make her putty in his hands. 'You are a very intelligent woman. I'm sure we can find many interesting ways to pass the time. Maybe...' his smile was piratical '... you should write them all down. I'd hate for us to miss anything out.'

Anna had been expecting, if not bunting, her mother to be waiting for her, eager for details. The year before Sancia left she would wait for Anna to get in from her dates with Ed, her painfully serious if very sweet sixth-form boyfriend. Sancia was desperate to be a cool, modern mother, to talk birth control and share confidences. Anna's refusal to disclose anything—not that there had been anything to disclose—had obviously disappointed her. At times Anna had been tempted to make up some torrid details just to make her mother happy.

Of course, when she'd needed her mother, when Sebastian had walked away and broken her heart, when her life was such a mess she couldn't see any way to make it right, her mother had already left for La Isla Marina and Anna had realised just how alone she was, that her pain was hers alone. Her father was so emotionally remote, and she'd wanted to spare Rosa the burden of growing up too soon, a burden she knew all too well. In some ways she didn't think she would ever forgive Sancia for not being there.

To her surprise the jetty was empty, no casually hovering figure awaited her return and when she walked back to the villa she saw no one other than Maria.

It was still early, the air refreshing, but with a sultry tinge that suggested a scorching day ahead. At least the paint would dry quickly. Anna tried not to grimace at the thought of all the work still ahead of her. She'd had an afternoon and evening playing hooky; that would have to be enough for now.

The back of the villa opened out into a beautiful stone courtyard, hung about with trellises, plants and huge tubs of bright flowers, the view to the shore uninterrupted. The courtyard was home to the island's more informal restaurant and breakfast was also served *al-fresco* on the wrought-iron little tables and chairs. The handful of staff, Anna, Leo and her mother had fallen into the habit of congregating there first thing for freshly fried *churros*, served with rich, melted chocolate, fresh fruit and coffee. Anna swung round the side of the villa heading for the unmistakeable smell of the sweet fried dough only to skid to a halt. One of the tables was occupied by a man who definitely hadn't been there yesterday. Around the same age as Anna, he was pale with dark hair and, she couldn't help noticing, incredibly sexy.

Not as sexy as Leo, of course. Anna didn't have that same instinctive pull that had gravitated her towards Leo the day they met; she noted it more in an objective way. His attractiveness was part of him, effortless, something to admire like a painting or a song. Sancia would be beside herself, Anna thought, grinning, two gorgeous young men to chat up.

Nodding a greeting at the unknown man—although she couldn't help noting that he seemed awfully familiar—Anna looked around for her mother, blinking, then blinking again. Was she seeing things? 'Dad? What are you doing here?'

Was that really her father? Wearing shorts of all things, sitting at a table, *churros* in front of him, a coffee in hand, as if he had no cares or responsibilities in the world? And why was her mother sitting next to him, an excited warm smile on her face, one hand proprietorially on his arm? Had she actually sailed back into a different reality, one where her parents had not only never separated, but were actually happy?

'Your father arrived last night. He was worried about me. Isn't that sweet?'

Anna stared at her mother, trying to process her words through her admittedly tired brain. 'I didn't know you guys even talked,' she said lamely.

'I was worried when you abandoned your classes and work,' her father said. 'When your mother told me how much she has to do, I thought I'd offer my help.' Her parents shared an oddly conspiratorial look and unease whispered through Anna. What weren't they telling her?

'Oh.' So many conflicting replies flitted through Anna's mind she had no idea where to start. 'What use will you be? We need someone practical,' warred with, 'How have you not noticed how lost I am? Why do you never try and help *me*?' In the end she settled for, 'I just did you an online shop. I'd better see if I can cancel it.'

Her father gave no indication of having heard and, not for the first time, Anna couldn't help wondering if Rosa was right. If Anna should just let him try and look after himself; he wasn't just a grown man, he was a highly intelligent man, more than capable of remembering to take his pills and buy his own food. Probably. Anna narrowed her eyes. 'Hang on, didn't you have an appointment two days ago? What did the specialist say?' How could she have forgotten? She always accompanied her father, if only to make sure he actually obeyed the doctor's strictures.

The shifty look on her father's face told her everything she needed to know. 'She told you to rest, didn't she?' That was why he was here, not because he wanted to help, or had noticed that Anna was struggling, but to add to the workload.

'She said a change of scene might be helpful, that I could do with some sun and fresh air,' he admitted.

'Now, *querida*, don't nag your father.' Sancia stood up and her hand brushed the back of Anna's father's neck. 'We should just be glad that he's here, that Rosa will be here in less than a week and the whole family will be together. It's all too *maravilloso*!'

'Oh, yes, completely wonderful.' Was it too late for Anna to return to the boat and to instruct Leo to sail away anywhere but here and not come back? 'And who is your companion, Dad?'

'Hmm?' Professor Gray looked around as if a companion might have materialised on the spot beside him.

'Right there,' Anna whispered fiercely. 'Eating breakfast.'

'Oh, I never saw him before yesterday. We got the boat over together. He's staying here.'

'What?' Anna turned to her mother, eyebrows

raised so high she could feel the strain in her forehead. 'I didn't think we had anyone booked in. How long is he staying?'

'Jude? Just a few weeks.' Sancia waved her hand as if to indicate that time didn't matter. 'He knows we're not fully open yet, but that's what he wants. Peace and quiet and some inspiring scenery.'

'A few weeks? But Valentina's wedding is in just three weeks. He can't be here for that. She has reserved the whole island, remember?' Why was it Anna's responsibility to point this out? Years had passed, but nothing had changed.

'I know all this, *querida*. You really do worry too much. I've been running La Isla Marina for several years now. I do know how to sort out bookings. Jude is in Bungalow Five, that has been painted and according to your list didn't need any further work. If he is still here during the wedding then I'm sure Valentina will be happy for such a handsome boy to be part of the festivities.'

Anna rubbed her forehead, pretty sure that the ache in her temples had very little to do with lack of sleep and an awful lot to do with her mother's whimsical management style. 'But we haven't got in the new bed linen or towels or any of the extras to dress the bungalows up yet.'

'Anna, people have been holidaying here for many years, many of them come year after year, and they are all very happy with the simple look of the bungalows. The beds are comfortable, the sheets are clean—it's the views and the sport they come for, not scented candles.'

'This wedding is different, you know that. Every guest spends their life taking pictures and posting them online.' But Anna was a little mollified by her mother's words. If the man had chosen to take his holidays in a semi-closed resort then he would just have to take them as they were, ladders, paintbrushes and all. She smiled over at him as he stood and nodded politely in the family's direction, before ambling out of the courtyard, probably in search of that peace and quiet. He did look awfully familiar. What had her mother called him? Jude? Recognition teased her brain, but Anna still couldn't place him.

Rubbing her forehead again, Anna tried to push her parents out of her mind. She wasn't going to micromanage her father's health or take on her mother's responsibilities, not this time. Better to think about last night, to dwell on every second of the most wonderful night she had ever had—and to remember that there were more to come.

Best of all she already knew how this ended. There would be no unwelcome surprises, no heart broken, just a mutual parting of the ways. She could wave her pirate off into the sunset and resume her normal life with no regrets. Maybe she should see if Leo could help with her headache. He was bound to have some inventive cure up his sleeve, or at least a foolproof way of taking her mind off it.

'Your father is actually really handy with a paintbrush.' Leo leaned close to Anna as he spoke, enjoying the way she quivered as he touched her. Her hand crept into his as she leaned into him. Although he had no intention of analysing why, these moments were the highlight of Leo's day, the moments when they paused in their labours and simply gravitated towards each other. Luckily it was a small island, easy for Leo to track Anna down with minimal effort. Today she'd been helping her dad. Leo couldn't help noticing how reversed their roles seemed, Anna the patient parent with a particularly forgetful child. But he also saw the deep-rooted affection between them.

The same affection was evident between Anna and Sancia, despite Anna's issues with her mother. The last few days had been like living in the middle of a family—a quirky family, a family with problems, but a family with heart. Leo couldn't help wondering what it would be like to have parents he could tease, parents he could laugh with. Parents who loved him.

'Who would have thought it? I've never seen him do anything even remotely practical before. I didn't know he had it in him. What's more,' she added, 'I know it's only been a few days, but he looks a lot better than he has done for a long time, more relaxed, pink rather than that awful grey face I'm so used to seeing. I know how he feels. Despite all the cleaning and painting it's actually pretty peaceful here.'

'Enjoy every moment because it all changes tomorrow.' Leo wasn't looking forward to the influx of people due onto the island over the next couple of days, even though it would mean his own workload would be considerably lessened. The seasonal staff were all due and tomorrow the professional joiner, plumber and builders arrived to do a week's intensive work sorting out any jobs that had been beyond Leo, Anna and the groundsman. Not that their own workload would lessen too much, as Anna kept reminding him: the barmen would need help getting the three bars back up to scratch, the lifeguard would need a hand painting the boats and kayaks—and all fifty-two bungalows would need a post-repair intensive clean and to be dressed up in media-filter-friendly luxury. Every item ticked off on one of Anna's lists just seemed to generate another three. It seemed impossible that they would ever be done in time.

Leo had fully expected to be bored by now, to find an excuse to slope off for a few days' recuperation, but the combination of work and Anna kept him on the island. It wasn't all work either, he reflected as he ran his hand over her denim-clad hip. One of the tennis courts was in perfect condition, the sea was warming up nicely and the island's surfboards, windsurfs and pedal boats were all completely seaworthy. And of course there was Anna… Leo's throat dried as she pushed back against him, in a way he was sure she knew full well was calculated to drive him mad. Their agreement was working out very well. He wasn't at all ready to cut his losses, not nearly.

It would all feel so very different tomorrow. He now realised what an idyll the last two weeks had been, and how much he had needed it. Time out from his life, purpose.

'I can't believe that they start arriving so soon.' Anna's melancholy tone showed she shared his thoughts about the incoming invasion. 'We need them all, goodness knows, but I like it as we are. And Mama is expecting Rosa any day now.'

'You're not looking forward to seeing her? I know you're not close, but with your parents getting on so well…'

'Getting on suspiciously well, don't you think? They're always whispering in corners and I have no idea where Dad is sleeping, thank goodness. There are things no child needs to be privy to. And no, I don't see Rosa and I falling on each other's necks. I'm actually dreading it,' Anna confessed. 'She always brings out the worst in me. I get all defensive and prickly. I don't want you to see that side of me.'

'Then let's not be here when she gets here,' Leo suggested. 'You've left enough instructions for everyone to know what needs doing, and your father is more than capable of issuing out tools and work lists. I need to go to Barcelona to finalise the menu and instructions with the restaurant there. Come with me.'

'I can't just go off to Barcelona when there's so much to be done.' But she sounded tempted.

'Sure you can. In fact you should. The food is going to be absolutely key to the success of the wedding.'

She stilled under his embrace. 'It is, isn't it? You're right. When do we go?'

'Right now?'

'Now?'

'Look how well it turned out last time you decided to be spontaneous,' Leo said and she tapped his hand.

'The jury's still out on that one, thank you very much. How do you want to get there? Sail?'

'If only, but it would take us a few days. One

day I think we should set off for a long sail with no distractions, but this is not that day. No, we shall fly. Can you be ready in a couple of hours? Oh, and, Anna? Bring something dressy. We'll hit the town tonight.'

CHAPTER NINE

COMING HOME WAS always bittersweet. On one hand Leo loved Barcelona, the city where he had first tasted freedom, where he had started his business, where he had got to know Valentina. On the other it was irredeemably tainted by his upbringing at the old *castillo* just a few miles out of the city environs. Even though Leo maintained an apartment in one of the modernist buildings that characterised the ancient, proud city, he rarely stayed there.

Truth was his life was so contained he could manage on his boat or in a hotel with little difficulty. All he needed was his laptop and a few changes of clothes; his music was digitalised, his books likewise. His living spaces were a stark contrast to the antique-filled *castillo*, all of which were strictly for looking at, not touching—including many of the toys.

Anna's initial enthusiasm to see his 'inner

sanctum' as she termed it visibly dimmed when she set foot inside the huge apartment with its tiled floors and arched roof. Although she was clearly charmed by the many quirky modernist touches, by the huge terrace, the view out over the city and the leafy inner courtyard, she was much less enamoured of his sparse furnishings. 'This could be the most gorgeous apartment in the world,' she said after completing her tour. 'The bathroom is so perfect I want to move in and never leave, and as for the views...utterly incredible. But I've seen chain hotel rooms with more personality.'

'What can I say? I missed interior design week at school,' Leo tried to joke, passing her a freshly made gin and tonic and doing his best to steer her out to the terrace where the view more than made up for any deficiencies in the décor.

'It's just I don't see *you* in here.'

That could be because there was nothing of him to put into the apartment. Sometimes Leo thought that he and the old building had a lot in common—illustrious pedigrees housing something hollow.

Luckily it was easy to distract Anna with a

tour of the city and she was obviously enchanted by the parks, by the wonderful array of Gaudí buildings topped off with the still not finished Sagrada Família, and by the tapas served with their drinks in the small, local bars. 'Don't eat too many,' he warned her as she tucked into the small bowl of spicy *patatas bravas*. 'We've got an entire wedding menu to sample yet.'

Her hand stilled, hovering in mid-air over the small fried potatoes, topped with a spicy tomato sauce. 'I love tapas,' she said dreamily.

'Keep that thought in your head,' Leo advised her. 'There are a lot of dishes to sample. You might never want to eat them again when we finish.'

But Anna was shaking her head. 'Never going to happen.'

She was right. Despite the magnitude of the task before them she didn't seem daunted. The restaurant occupied the bottom floor of one of Gaudí's distinctive curvy buildings and Anna and Leo were seated in the private dining room, a cave-like alcove with undulating walls and a colourful mosaic on the ceiling. The room could seat up to twelve people, but it didn't feel too big for two, not when the table was set with a huge variety of bowls and plates, each with a card propped up against it with the name of the dish written neatly on.

'Right.' Leo handed Anna a pen and a menu. 'Tick the ones you like best. Be sparing with your samplings though. This is just the first round.'

'You're going to have to wheel me out of here, or maybe roll me out.' But she didn't sound at all worried by the task ahead. 'This is my type of research. Why didn't I decide to write about the history of food in Barcelona rather than boring old queens? I'm sure I'd be much further along with the book-from-hell than I am now.'

Leo waited until she had filled her plate with a selection of stuffed olives, marinated anchovies and meatballs before taking his seat and pouring her a glass of wine. 'You don't seem very enthused by your current work,' he commented. When he had first met Anna he might have poked fun at her job, but secretly he'd been impressed. She had a real passion, something she was an expert in. Academia would never make her the kind of money that speculation and investment made Leo, but she was far richer in all the ways that mattered.

Yet all her enthusiasm seemed reserved for her older work. Every time Anna mentioned her new book, her forehead creased, a pinch of worry visible at the bridge of her nose, some self-deprecating comment ready.

'I am,' she said quickly. 'It's just a lot of pressure, that's all. We need to publish all the time, to build our reputations, to seal the university's reputation. And of course what we publish has to be really innovative and groundbreaking.'

'Like a feminist reinterpretation proving the sanity of Joanna the Mad?'

There it was, the enthusiasm missing from any conversations about her current book. Anna's eyes were immediately alight, the meatball on the end of her fork in danger of falling as she gesticulated widely. 'Poor Joanna, she had a really hard life. Every man in her life betrayed her, you know, her father, husband, brother, son. Then she was sent to a convent for the rest of her life. She was probably a little unhinged by all that, as any of us would be. That book was considered groundbreaking, although some people,' she added darkly, 'don't think it counts as research. They don't think that anything that's shelved in popular history and actually sells more than three copies can be academic enough to count. Other people think I'm all hype...'

'Hype?'

'I was only twenty-six when it came out, and the publishers went for this really moody black and white author photo, all bare shoulders and loose hair, playing on my Spanish heritage. It was a little controversial amongst my peers. When I got invited onto TV and radio to do interviews, and to book festivals, there was a lot of nasty talk. That I traded on Dad's reputation—which, despite his inability to remember to take his own medicine, is stellar—that I used my looks to get ahead. That I was a one-book wonder.'

'They were jealous.'

'Yes, but there is just enough truth in the accusations to sting. The photo probably *was* a little too sexy, and my name certainly didn't hold me back. Truth was I liked the photo, liked the image they created. That Anna looks fearless, so sure of herself. I just wish she was real.'

Leo had never heard her sound quite so self-doubting before. All he wanted to do was show Anna that she was wrong, that she was more than the success of one book. He swallowed, hand tightening on his fork. This overpowering need to comfort, to help, was uncharted territory, terrifying in its vastness. He fought to sound light, almost uninterested. 'Does it matter that much? If you don't write another groundbreaking book. After all, most of us don't even manage to write one.'

'Does it matter?' She stared at him, eyes huge with astonishment. 'Of course it matters. My reputation, my career, they are all I have. If I'm not an eminent historian then who am I? What have I achieved? What was it all for?'

Leo waited until the first courses had been cleared away and an array of seafood arranged before them—crispy, delicate fried calamari, prawns glistening with garlic and olive oil, sweet clams served with artichokes, and salt cod fritters, the whole thing served with a delicious selection of salads, rice and fresh bread. It all looked incredible, but his appetite had gone, chased away by the tumult in his mind. Why did he care so much about how Anna felt? They were just keeping each other company, turning what could be a dull few weeks into something more entertaining. Moreover, they were totally chalk and cheese. She was fun to be with in the short term—the very short term—but that organised, note-taking, sensible nature would drive him mad before too long.

His lifestyle might be a charade, but he was still used to pleasing no one but himself, his own needs, desires and whims paramount. Maybe it was selfish, but at least this way he could do no damage. He took a sip of wine and searched for a safe topic of conversation. 'What's the new book about?'

Anna didn't answer at once, busy staring at a huge prawn with fascinated wonder. She closed her eyes as she bit into it. 'Ohmigod, that is absolutely amazing. Tick this dish, several times.' She took another bite, swallowing slowly, eyes still closed.

'Do you want me to give you and the *gambas* some privacy?'

'Yes please, all I need is some music, candle-light and a plate of these bad boys.' She speared another prawn with a flourish. 'So, my new book is also about Spanish queens, not consorts, but rulers. It seemed to make sense, you know, after Joanna did so well. Unluckily for me the Spanish haven't been too keen on female monarchs, so I only have Isabella I of Ferdinand and Isabella fame, and then a mere three hundred years later another Isabella, Isabella II as she is originally known. They shared more than a name. They both had to struggle to be recognised as rulers in their own right; they lived in times of great uncertainty and change. But all I have is a series of anecdotes, a lot of dates. Nothing more than a plain biography. I can't see my way through to something new.' She looked at the prawns speculatively, before pushing the plate away.

'Then pick another topic.'

'It's not that easy. My editor, my agent, my college have all approved this. I've dedicated the last two years to research. I have an advance, a contract...'

Leo sat back. 'What drew you to Joanna in the first place?'

Anna paused, her eyes soft in the dim light. 'My grandmother used to tell me bedtime stories about her. The traditional ones, you know, the "carting her husband's corpse all over the country" one. I wanted to find out more.'

'So it was the story that attracted you, not finding something groundbreaking?'

Anna paused, laying her fork on the plate in front of her. 'I guess.'

'There you are. Look for the story first and then look for the facts. Find a story which sings to you.'

'I'm a historian, not a storyteller.' But she looked thoughtful.

Leo picked up his glass of wine. 'Can't you be both?'

Leo's words continued to echo around Anna's mind as they finished the seafood and moved on to meat and vegetables before finishing with a final course of sweet dishes and a platter of cheese and fruit. She'd always known who she was and what she wanted to be. But why? Because her father noticed her when she got top marks in history, liked her following in his footsteps?

No. Or at least, she conceded, not wholly. She

had always loved the stories behind the facts, loved bringing the long-dead back to life with her words. Maybe Leo was right. Maybe she was looking in the wrong place at the wrong stories. All she knew was that she couldn't put off calling her agent any longer. Her book needed a profound rethink, maybe even her entire career. Just coming to that conclusion was like losing a huge burden she hadn't even known she carried, she was so used to the weight.

She smiled at Leo, but he didn't notice, sunk in thought, barely touching the incredible food, his shoulders a little slumped. Was his mood due to being back in Barcelona? He'd mentioned his parents lived just outside the city.

What would it be like to despise your parents? Anna freely admitted that hers exasperated her, frequently disappointed her, but she loved them, recognising that their flaws were a crucial part of them. She even envied them, wished she could have a little of her mother's insouciance, her father's certainty. Leo didn't mention his parents often but when he did anger was never far from the surface—and buried underneath the desolation of someone lost.

Maybe that was why his apartment was so impersonal, why he preferred to spend his time on his boat, never anchored down. He didn't know where he belonged.

The urge to fix him was almost overwhelming. But Anna had tried fixing people in the past. Tried to fix her father's health, her mother's unhappiness, her sister. She'd failed all three. The truth was she couldn't fix anyone who didn't want to be fixed. And that kind of involvement wasn't part of their deal anyway. She had to remember what their friendship was, remember what happened last time she'd started projecting feelings onto another human being, seeing truths that simply weren't there.

'Thank you,' she said, sliding, with some difficulty, off the bench. 'How many dishes did we tick?'

'You ticked nearly all of them,' Leo said with a ghost of a smile. 'Luckily I was a little more restrained.'

'They were all delicious. Do you know, now the decorations have arrived, now we've discussed the practicalities with the kitchen here, now the rest of the staff are due to arrive, I'm beginning to think maybe, just maybe, we can pull this wedding off after all.'

'I always knew you could do it.' The intensity in his dark eyes weakened her knees. 'The minute I met you, when you marched up to me, notebook in hand, wanting my name, rank and badge number. I almost saluted.'

'You did not. You were arrogant and supercilious, and downright annoying.' And sexy as hell, but she wasn't going to admit that.

'All I wanted to do was unbutton you. In every possible way,' Leo said hoarsely and Anna had to grip the table to prevent her legs from buckling, heat spreading from the pit of her stomach, scorching a path along every nerve.

She licked her lips, desperate for moisture in her suddenly dry mouth. 'How's that going for you?'

'I'd say not too bad. There's some ways to go…'

'Really?' She arched a brow, aiming for cool and casual, but all too aware of her heart hammering away.

'I'm just waiting till I have your full attention, *mi cariño*.'

The promise in his voice turned her insides molten, her grip tightening on the table. 'You have it.' Was that really her voice? So husky, so full of desire? How could Leo seduce her so completely with nothing more than words and eyes full of promise? Her whole body was pulsing with desire, swaying towards his as if he was her true north, her true south, her everything.

'No, part of you is still wondering what's going on on La Isla Marina, another part of you is thinking about your book, and I'm pretty sure you are still obsessing over those prawns. My task will be completed when you can think of nothing but me. Nothing but me and what I'm going to do to you.'

The noise that escaped her was purely involuntary, a mix between a gasp of surprise and a moan of pure need. The smug smile that spread across his face showed he'd achieved his goal. No way, she vowed, would Leo di Marquez get to have everything his own way. Summoning all her strength, Anna stepped forward, her eyes focussed directly on his.

'That's nothing compared to what I'm going to do to you before this is through,' she said.

'Consider this a challenge. And, Leo? Remember how much I like to win.'

Surprise flared in his eyes, wiping the slightly smug expression off his face. Surprise swiftly replaced by lust so pure it was as if the whole room seemed to smoulder with its heat. 'Challenge accepted.' He stepped back. 'I think we should go back to the apartment, An-na.' His voice lingered lovingly over her name. 'Don't you?'

He didn't take her hand as they exited the room, barely looked at her as they bid farewell to the manager, Leo promising to email the final menu choices through the next day. He didn't need to. They were connected by a rope of desire, binding them together, ensuring she was aware of his every move, every word, moving with him like the steps of an ancient dance. This wasn't what she'd signed up for. This went beyond a good time, crossing a barrier she knew neither of them were ready to cross and yet they had no choice. It felt foreordained and she welcomed her fate, however it fell.

The formalities over, they walked slowly, in perfect time towards the door. There was no need to hurry. They might as well savour every single second of this night. Somehow Anna already knew it would be the kind of night she would relive in her dreams, the kind of night she would look back on as on old lady and know that she had lived.

'Leo?' A sharp, surprised voice cut through the atmosphere that surrounded them and Leo halted, a curiously blank expression immediately descending onto his face. The deep breath he took was so quick Anna might have thought she'd imagined it, if she hadn't seen his hands curl into quick, tight fists before relaxing again.

He turned, slowly, and looked at the corner table where a well-heeled couple sat. 'Madre, Padre. What a surprise.' He'd switched to Spanish, she realised. Her own was fluent enough that the transition wasn't too much of a problem, although he immediately reverted to English. 'I'd like you to meet Dr Anna Gray. Anna, these are my parents, the Conde and Condessa de Olvares.'

Should she curtsey? It almost seemed as if the haughty woman, her hair in the kind of sleek chignon Anna could never manage, her outfit a marvel of devastating understatement and wealth, expected it. Anna reined in the urge, smiling instead. *'Encantado,'* she said with a nod instead. 'Leo has told me so much about you. It's a pleasure to meet you.'

There was no answering smile, just a swift, sweeping look, which quite clearly summed Anna up, found her wanting and dismissed her. All in less than three seconds. Impressive.

'How long are you back?' The Conde had at least switched to English, even if he didn't acknowledge Anna outright, his cold attention focussed on his son.

'One night only.'

'How lucky we ran into you, then.'

'Lucky indeed.'

'Please, join us for a coffee and a drink.' His sharp gaze switched to Anna. 'If it's agreeable to your companion? We so rarely get the pleasure of our only son's company.'

'Coffee will be lovely,' Anna said as the silence stretched on.

Leo didn't react in any way and she couldn't tell if her acceptance annoyed him or not. He stood, unmoving, a beat too long for comfort and then inclined his head. 'How can I turn down such a civil invitation?'

'You've been very quiet, Leo,' his mother said once their plates had been removed and coffee and brandy supplied to the whole table. Anna rarely drank spirits, but she clutched her glass gladly, aware she needed some help to get her through the next few minutes. 'I don't think I've seen your picture in the paper for months.'

'How are you making ends meet? Don't tell me you're looking for a job? More than time you settled down, in every way.' The Conde swirled his brandy as he spoke.

'I've been doing this and that. In fact, right now I'm working with my hands. That's how I met Anna. She's employed me to do some painting and decorating, haven't you, Dr Gray?'

'I wouldn't say employed.'

'Bed and board only. Still, I'm grateful.' Leo lounged elegantly, his own glass in one hand, turning it into the light.

'Leo's very kindly helping out.' Anna didn't know why she was trying to explain, why she was once again taking up the mantle of peacemaker, a mantle she had worn through most of her childhood. 'I'd be lost without him.' The last bit was true enough.

'Señor di Marquez, you're still here?' At this opportune moment the manager bustled up, phone in hand. 'One more thing I need to confirm. Señorita Valentina has asked for a small discount in return for the attention generated by her forthcoming wedding. We don't usually court such publicity, and as you know we have little need to advertise, but as Señorita Valentina is a well-loved daughter of the city and we wish her all the best for her wedding, we are happy to acquiesce on this occasion. I hope the *señorita* will be happy with the final quote.'

Anna couldn't help watching the Conde and his wife's faces throughout the long-winded speech. Their usual expressions of bored condescension betrayed into a horrified surprise. The manager had no sooner backed away when the Conde rounded on his son.

'You're involved in that girl's wedding?'

'That girl is my sister.'

'Valentina's holding the wedding on the island my mother owns,' Anna interjected, not knowing whether she was making things better or worse, just knowing she needed to defuse the rapidly building tension. 'It's going to be very traditional, but very beautiful, I think.'

'And she would like you there.' Leo gazed steadily at his father. '*Dios* knows why, but she does.' And then, when the Conde failed to respond, 'She has asked me to accompany her down the aisle.'

'What?' The exclamation came from the Condessa and, glancing over, Anna saw her knuckles were white.

'She wants a male member of her family to walk with her.'

'This nonsense has gone on long enough!' Anna stared at the Conde. She had never seen such palpable yet controlled anger. The Conde hadn't raised his voice, no one looking over would guess that this was anything but a cordial discussion, yet the air throbbed with his rage. Was this how Leo had been raised? Under this measured anger?

'You are a disgrace to the family name, to your mother and to me. Your life is frivolous and meaningless, your friends worthless and your insistence on flaunting your relationship with that girl an embarrassment. It stops now, Leo. You will return to the *castillo* with your mother and I, get a proper job, start shouldering some of your responsibilities and marry someone suitable. Do you understand me?'

'And if I don't?'

Anna couldn't believe the nonchalance in Leo's voice, didn't believe his father's outburst hadn't affected him, no matter how easily he lounged, how amused his smile.

'I'll disinherit you. You'll get the title, but nothing else.'

Leo didn't bat as much as an eyelash. 'Such a shame the inheritance laws preclude you from doing that. But don't worry, Padre, I don't need a penny of your money.'

'I find that hard to believe. Oh, you may scrape by, sponging off your friends and gambling, but don't tell me you're not short of money, a wastrel like you.'

That was it. She'd heard enough. 'I have only known Leo a few weeks, but I knew within a week that he was so much more than he portrayed himself to be. And I am ashamed, *ashamed*,' she repeated, proud that her voice wasn't wobbling, 'that it took me that long. I was prejudiced, I admit. But I should have seen within the first hour just what a good, loyal man he is. Just how principled he is. How hardworking. It took me a week. But you? You have had a lifetime and you still don't see him at all. Shame on you.' Anna pushed her still-undrunk brandy away and got to her feet. 'Thank you for the drink. Leo? I believe we have unfinished business to conclude. I wish I could say it was nice meeting you both, but I was brought up to be honest.'

And without looking to see if her words had any effect, without looking to see if Leo was following her, Anna swept out of the restaurant.

CHAPTER TEN

LEO KNEW THAT when he looked back on this moment he'd regret not taking the time to enjoy the identical shocked expressions on his parents' faces. But all he could do was get to his feet, nod to them politely and follow Anna out of the restaurant, thoughts and feelings whirling so fast he was amazed he could walk in a straight line.

No one had ever spoken about him with such passion, such tenderness, such understanding before. Leo was used to disdain, used to amusement, used to contempt. Understanding was beyond him and, he suspected, when he processed how he felt about Anna's intervention he would be undone—which was why he wasn't going to process it just now.

Anna stood waiting outside the restaurant, her expression anxious. 'I'm sorry. I shouldn't have…'

Tilting her chin, Leo stared into her eyes for

one long second, drinking in the still-simmering anger mixed with contrition before bending his head to hers and kissing her. Hard. It wasn't the seductive kiss he had planned, not a teasing romantic gesture. It was passion, gratitude, need, lust all mixed together in one intoxicating mixture—and she kissed him back equally fiercely, her hands snaking into his hair, pulling him closer and closer until they were almost fused into one.

'Let's go back,' he breathed finally, reluctant to break the contact, and Anna nodded. But he couldn't let her go, not yet, his arm around her shoulders holding her close. Leo didn't usually hold hands with anyone, but tonight he wanted everyone to know the blue-eyed girl in the demure black dress belonged with him. To him.

'I didn't mean to say anything,' Anna said after a moment, her arm tight around his waist. 'I hope I didn't make things worse.'

He laughed at that, low and deep. 'I don't think they could be made worse.'

Anna didn't join in the laughter. 'Why do they speak to you like that?'

'You heard them, my life is frivolous, a waste.

They see what they want to see. They catch a few photos, a few headlines and to them, that's the truth. I embarrass them, and if there is one thing my parents can't take it's public humiliation.'

'You do know that you're not the person they think you are, don't you? I meant every word I said in there.'

Did he? He tried to tell himself that, but somehow he never quite managed to convince himself. The intensity in Anna's voice went some way to soothing the pain in his soul. He tightened his grip on her waist. 'They've known me for thirty years. You've only known me for a couple of weeks...'

'I look for the truth behind the story, remember?' She stopped and turned towards him, her hands cupping his face as she looked into his eyes. 'You need to let them go, Leo. You need to move past them. Find a way to be happy.'

'If only it was that easy.'

'It's not, but I believe in you. Believe in yourself.'

Finally they reached his apartment building and Leo guided Anna up the three flights of stairs, their steps in perfect unison, hands clasped tight. Half an hour ago he had been anticipating this moment, this arrival back at the apartment, how charged the atmosphere would be between them, how ready they would be. He had planned to kick the door shut behind them, turn to her, capture her mouth, explore her body right there in his apartment hallway, couldn't imagine having the patience to carry her to the sofa, let alone the bedroom, passion thrumming so hard it was barely contained. The passion was still there, but the meeting with his parents had dimmed it somewhat, and he didn't want their eventual coming together to be tainted by anger and spite.

The doors to the terrace were still ajar and wordlessly they walked over, stepping through the doors, and leaned on the balustrade, staring out at the city below.

'I grew up thinking that my parents' approval was within my grasp,' Leo said eventually. 'I tried to be the perfect son, to not demand anything, to be no trouble, to make them proud, and yet they always went away again, I always messed up. Disappointed them. I broke something, didn't know my lessons well enough, wasn't still enough during Mass, talked at the theatre, didn't answer their friends' questions quickly enough. Whatever I did, no matter how hard I tried, I never lived up to their high expectations. I used to get sick when I knew they were due home, with excitement, with tension, promising myself this time would be different, that I wouldn't fail. But I always did.'

'It's not failing to be a child, to act like a child. You must see that now.'

'The thing is, Anna, it wasn't just them. Everyone went, everyone left, every maid, every nanny. No matter how small I tried to make myself, how good, it never worked.' He swallowed, memories bitter in his throat. 'I couldn't understand it. Then, when I was maybe about ten, after Valentina's mother had left, I heard my nanny talking to her friend. About me.'

Anna leaned in close, her warmth a balm to his soul. 'What did she say?'

Leo couldn't look at Anna, couldn't bear to see pity on her face. Or worse, agreement. 'That I was no trouble, but I was too quiet to be true. It was creepy, she said. I wasn't natural. There was something missing.' He took a deep breath, the memory of that night so clear it was as if he were still there, standing frozen by the door, the night falling, too stunned to move. That was the night his heart had broken, the night he had re-alised what was wrong with him. Realised why no one stayed, why no one loved him.

There was something missing.

'That's a terrible thing to say.'

'She was right though, wasn't she? There had to be a reason, Anna. Most parents don't ignore their only child. Most parents don't dislike their son, spend as much time away from him as pos-sible. It had to be me. I knew it, as soon as she spoke. Knew it was all my fault.'

'No.' Her voice was sharp as she turned to him. 'I wish I could tell you that every parent loves their child, that all childhoods are happy, but it isn't true, Leo. There's no test for new par-ents, no training. And some people are simply lousy parents. Through active cruelty, or neglect, or because they're too selfish to put their chil-dren first. Your parents made sure you were fed, looked after, educated, but they still neglected you. And that's on them, will always be on them, will never be on you. And shame on that nanny for not seeing it, for not helping you.'

What was that lump in his throat? That swelling in his chest? Leo swallowed, willing the surge of emotion away, not sure he could cope with the consequences if he allowed it to overwhelm him. All he could do was speak, carry on unburdening his soul to the bright-eyed girl next to him—although he knew he would regret his confidences by the time dawn lit the terrace. 'By the time I was eighteen I told myself I'd given up, but I hadn't, not really. I still wanted their approval. To be worth more than the continuation of a name, a title. But then I found out about Valentina… I'd spent all those years wanting to be someone my parents approved of, were proud of. Overnight I wanted the opposite. I wanted to shame them the way they shamed me.'

'Hence the pretence? Hiding behind your reputation?'

He nodded. 'Ironically my father showed me the way. He took me to a club on my eighteenth birthday. Men only, apart from the hostesses, men of breeding like us, men with money, power. The kind of man he expected me to be. Fortunes changed overnight at this club, men gambled, bought sex, took drugs, but, crucially, it was exclusive and therefore respectable. That was the first time he made it clear—all vices could be indulged as long as they were hidden, as long as publicly I followed the rules. I knew the only way to hurt him was to drag his precious name through the dirt as often, as wildly as I could.'

Anna moved a little closer, her arm brushing his, burning, branding him. 'How long did the novelty last?'

'Just a few weeks,' Leo confessed. 'I was bored within days. I had also promised Assumptia I would help them out so I got a job, on a building site. The son of the Conde de Olvares nothing but a common labourer by day, masquerading as a playboy by night. Luckily I made a small sum of money that very first time I went to a casino. I invested some of my profits in shares, and some in a business a friend was setting up. Both prospered and so I reinvested the profits and then again and again until I could give up the job and set up my own business.' It sounded so easy, as if it were luck, not maths and formulae, and business plans and gut instinct. 'There have been losses of course, failure, but generally I have been lucky.'

'And they still have no idea? What you really do?'

'None,' Leo confirmed. 'Truth is I stopped partying almost straight away, but the seeds were sown. I show my face at just enough parties, the odd famous casino and they believe the headlines and gossip columns. They think I live from one spin of the roulette wheel to the next when the reality is I could probably buy the family fortune twice over.'

'What about your trust fund?'

'There is no trust fund. Not until I settle down, run the family estates and marry. My parents keep hoping to starve me into submission. They've been waiting a long time. They'll wait a lot longer. I have no intention of giving them anything they want. I won't be taking over the family estates, I won't marry, I will never father an heir.' It wasn't just a case of thwarting his parents; what did Leo know of marriage, of love, of fatherhood? He saw Valentina, so fearless in her love for Todd, and envied her, even as he shrank from the trust she handed her fiancé along with her heart. Leo only trusted himself. It was safer that way.

'Don't let them take that away from you as well, Leo. They took your childhood. You should own the rest of your life. Be happy. Isn't that the best punishment for them? Your happiness?'

'I can't, Anna. I can't risk it. I don't know what happiness is—and I would never pass that legacy on to a child.'

'Oh, Leo.' Anna reached up, drew a finger down his cheek. He closed his eyes at the touch, so light and yet so very right. 'It must get very lonely being you.'

Leo paused, her words softly spoken and yet hitting him right in the heart. He didn't like to admit any weakness and loneliness was the biggest weakness of all. He was thirty, rich by any calculation, he could walk into any city in Europe and bump into an acquaintance, be invited to a party, surround himself with people. But, Valentina aside, who truly knew him?

And did Valentina even know him? He cast himself as her protector. Showed her no weakness. She needed that from him. Somehow Anna saw through all his defences, saw deep within him. That wasn't in their agreement, wasn't something he wanted and yet here they were.

No, these thoughts weren't for tonight. Tonight was the cityscape glittering below, the stars glittering overhead. Tonight was Anna, so close to him he could feel her breathing. He turned, his hands on her bare arms, and felt her quiver, the movement shuddering through him. 'Now then, Dr Gray,' he said softly and with satisfaction he watched her pupils flare, heard her breath hitch. 'We were in the middle of something when my parents so rudely interrupted us. Let's remind ourselves where we were, shall we?' Leo bent to kiss the hollow of her throat and as he tasted the soft saltiness of her skin the rest fell away. There was only her and for tonight there was nowhere else he would rather be.

It was late when Anna finally stretched and opened her eyes. The sun slatted in through the blinds, casting a warmth on the bed, the air already ripe with heat, but the space next to her was cool. Leo must have got up some time before. She sat up, pulling the sheet with her, wrapping it around herself, aware of her nakedness, here in this strange apartment in this strange city.

She shivered as memories of their lovemaking returned. The sex had been good—really good—from the start. Leo was a skilled and generous lover and the chemistry between them added an extra heat to their activities. But last night had been intense, almost dark at times, as if Leo had been trying to lose himself in her. As if she had been trying to heal him. But she knew that she couldn't heal him, the damage was too deep, too ingrained. Leo would have to try and heal himself. Only she was pretty sure he never would.

Why did the thought of that hurt her so much? Was it because the easy days and easier nights they had promised themselves had twisted into something darker? Or was it because she was beginning to forget her promise to herself not to fall for him?

'*Buenos dias.*'

'Morning.' She pulled the sheet higher, suddenly, unaccountably shy, brightening when she saw the paper cup in Leo's hand. 'Oh, coffee.'

'And pastries,' Leo confirmed, tossing a paper

bag onto the bed. 'And these...' Another bag followed the pastries. Anna grabbed it, her cheeks heating up when she saw the contents. 'I'd hate for us to run out. And the rate we're using them...'

'It's important to be safe,' Anna said with as much dignity as she could muster, putting the bag filled with packets of condoms back onto the bed.

'I expect nothing less from you. I'm surprised you haven't given me a list of ways to make sure we use them correctly.' She ducked her face at his teasing tone. 'Hey, what did I say?'

'Nothing. You're right. I do want to be safe.' She knew all too well the catastrophic consequences of taking a chance with contraception, how easily a spontaneous moment could ruin a life. She had no intention of repeating the same mistake, no matter how romantic the setting, how seductive the man. She looked up and forced a smile, but he wasn't fooled.

'What's wrong?'

'Nothing. I'm fine.' She grabbed the bag of pastries. 'These look amazing, thank you.'

Leo's eyes darkened. 'You don't have to tell

me, Anna, but neither do you have to pretend. Don't lie. Not to me. I thought we were honest with each other.'

He was right. She didn't have to tell him anything. But last night he had bared his soul to her. Didn't she owe him a secret in return? A balancing of the scales between them? 'I wasn't always careful,' she said eventually. 'I believed someone when he said it would be fine. Although I was old enough to know better. I just wanted to be the kind of person who took a risk. A different Anna.' She couldn't look at him, all her focus on the paper bag, the pastry crumbling under her nervous touch.

'There's nothing wrong with this Anna. You don't need to change a thing. And if he thought so then he didn't deserve you.'

The controlled anger in his voice steadied her, and for the first time in a long while Anna wanted to confide in someone. Maybe then she could finally heal. Finally move on. And this man who had shared so much with her, who she would never see again once their time was over, was here, asking for her trust. She swallowed, putting the pastries to one side and finally looking up to meet his eyes. 'His name was Sebastian. You remind me of him in some ways. He was rich, entitled, arrogant, supremely confident. I thought he was Mr Darcy and every Georgette Heyer rake and Lord Peter Wimsey all rolled into one.'

'Is he the man you fell in love with?'

He'd remembered. 'The man I was so infatuated with,' she corrected him. 'I'd spent my whole life being careful, Leo. Sensible. Things were great when I was little. Dad found Mama's scattiness endearing, and Mama loved the way he looked after her. But at some point they stopped being amused by each other. Rosa was still small, so I stepped into the role of peacemaker. I tried to make sure things were organised at home so Dad wouldn't get cross, to cover up for Mama. I was so used to doing it that when she left I just carried on. I didn't even leave home when I started university, still looking after Rosa, not that she wanted me to, or thanked me for it. And then I met Sebastian.' Her voice faltered.

'Your knight in shining armour?'

'He swept me off my feet. Truth was he was unreliable, could behave appallingly, but I thought I could reform him. I might have been book-smart, but when it came to men I was a naïve fool. For three months I followed him around like a lapdog, did everything he wanted, never allowed myself to question how he treated me, how he acted with other people. Told myself I was living a more glamorous, exciting life, even though at heart I think his arrogant disdain for people not as privileged as him made me uncomfortable. Then I forgot to be careful…'

'You got pregnant?'

'I got pregnant.' She stared at the sheet, remembering how terrified she had been, and yet so hopeful. Even excited. 'I stupidly thought it might all be fine. That he loved me and that we could make a life together, that he would welcome me into his gilded world. Truth was he was already bored. I just didn't want to see it. He walked away. A month later I miscarried.' She took a deep breath as the memory of the darkness swirled through her mind. 'I went to pieces. Blamed myself for it all. It took me a long time to get my life back, to forgive myself. I swore

I would never be that foolish, that gullible, that reckless ever again.'

She took a deep breath. Last night she had wanted Leo to face some unpalatable truths; now it was time to face some of her own. 'That time left its scars. I nearly lost my place at university, so I dug in, hid behind my studies. Became a scholar because I didn't know who else to be, didn't trust myself, trust my judgement. Told myself Dad needed me to stay at home. Truth is I needed him just as much. More.'

Leo sat down next to her, taking her hand in his. 'You're so brave, Anna, a survivor.'

'I'm not.' Was that really what he saw?

'Brave, dangerous, compassionate. I'm so sorry that happened to you. That he happened to you.'

'It was a long time ago.' But she had been living with the consequences ever since, hiding away, behind her book, her title, her father's illness. Who would she be if Sebastian hadn't tainted her life?

Anna had no idea, but maybe it was time she found out.

CHAPTER ELEVEN

ANNA HEADED TOWARDS the villa, unable to believe it was time for the final checklist. Thanks to all the outside help and some truly Herculean efforts by the staff, every bungalow was ready. Fresh paint gleamed white in the late spring sun, the shutters and doors a fresh green contrast. The outside areas were all weeded, the greenery trimmed back to lush from jungle-like, and new cushions and umbrellas had been added to the cleaned and repaired outside tables. Inside looked just as good, every bungalow scrubbed surgically clean and dressed with new gossamer-thin white curtains, fresh white cotton bedding, crockery and artfully arranged mirrors and flower arrangements, keeping the look as simple as possible while adding the luxurious feel Valentina and her guests would expect from their living quarters. More importantly every toilet flushed, every shower worked perfectly and there wasn't a single dripping tap anywhere on the island.

Although the guests could order food at any of the island's three bars or two restaurants at any time of the day or night, Anna had also stocked the tiny kitchenettes with coffee machines and a range of exclusive herbal teas. Work was still continuing on the public areas, the last few boats and kayaks needed to be checked, the third tennis court to be resurfaced and Anna was still waiting for the cushions and throws she had ordered for the biggest bar, but the beach bars were rethatched and restocked, the breakfast courtyard was ready for their guests' arrival, and the pagoda and central courtyard where the wedding and reception were to be held were nearly ready, fairy lights already strung through the surrounding trees.

They'd done a good job, she and Leo. Anna smiled just at the thought of his name, even though she knew she was heading for a fall. Attraction had turned to lust to trust and now she was already in far, far too deep, but she couldn't, wouldn't get out now even if someone threw her a lifeline.

She leaned against the doorframe to steady herself. God help her she was falling in love with Leo di Marquez. It was beyond foolish and she had no doubt it would end in her heartbreak, but some things were just meant to be and for once she wasn't going to borrow trouble, she was going to enjoy every minute she had with Leo and let the future take care of itself.

But one thing she knew was absolute: Leo mustn't know. She wasn't his salvation, this wannabe bad boy's redemption. They had made an agreement and she was going to stick to it. The only person to break her heart this time would be Anna herself. She had sworn that nobody else would ever have that power over her again.

'You're looking all doe-eyed. Does Señor Tall, Dark and Handsome have anything to do with that?' A sardonic voice from the office made Anna stop and grit her teeth. They'd arrived back on La Isla Marina to find Rosa had breezed onto the island while they had gone and, true to form, was already right at home—Anna had seen her sister in a couple of intense conversations with their mysterious guest from which she'd emerged with flushed cheeks and sparkling eyes. It never took her sister much time to stake out her territory.

Not, Anna reflected, that it had taken too much time for *her* to get close to Leo. Not that her sister needed to know that. She smiled as sweetly as she could. 'None of your business.'

Rosa appeared at the office door and Anna's teeth ground down even harder. How did her sister manage to look so effortlessly cool no matter what she was wearing? Her thick dark hair might look like Anna's to the untrained eye, but Anna had never managed to get the hang of braids, let alone the thick fishtail plait Rosa had confined her glossy tresses in, strands hanging just so, as if it had been designed by some boho hairdressing genius. She was casual in jeans and a T-shirt, but still managed to look chic enough to walk into the ritziest party, Anna's own shorts and T-shirt suddenly looking dowdy by comparison.

'How's the paperwork? Sorted out the wedding guests into rooms yet?'

It was Rosa's turn to set her jaw. 'I don't understand why you're being so stubborn. You love spreadsheets and solving problems. I love being outside and fixing things. We should just swap...'

'If you'd hadn't arrived over two weeks late then you could have had your pick of jobs. As it was I had to get on and do what needed doing most. You keep going with the wedding planning and helping Mama with the office. It'll do you good to stretch yourself.' Back then Anna would have jumped at the chance to swap responsibilities with Rosa, now she wanted to see the repairs and decorating through, proud of what she and Leo had achieved.

'Of course you dropped everything and rushed straight here.' The scorn in her sister's voice hit Anna right in the gut, just where it always did.

'It's a good thing I did. Look at what your *stand back and let them make their own mistake*s plan has achieved. This place was chaos...'

'Chaos until St Anna turned up and fixed it all?'

'Yes. Actually.' Besides, Rosa had turned up eventually; she must have felt a little guilty to have put her plans to one side.

'Dragging Dad with you? Couldn't trust him on his own for a month?'

'Dad turned up on his own.' Anna folded her arms. 'You do know he nearly died?' she said almost conversationally.

'What?' The smug look disappeared off Rosa's face. 'Nonsense, he looks fine.'

'He looks fine now. He looks fine because he has no stress outside work, his meals are prepared, he takes his pills, he gets reminded to take regular walks. Not because I'm a saint, not because I'm a martyr, but because someone has to do it—and no.' Anna raised her hand as Rosa tried to interrupt. 'Don't tell me he's an adult, I know that. I also know that when he wants to be he's the most organised man alive. But his health isn't a priority, work is. And he would forget, just like Mama forgot to take care of the basics here. So what do I do, Rosa? Swan off to Harvard and let him get ill and Mama sink? Is that your answer?' The offer for a semester at the prestigious university had recently been renewed, not that Anna had allowed herself to consider it, worry over her book, over her father making the move an impossibility.

'I don't understand.' Rosa paled—as much as she could with a truly enviable tan. 'I was ten before I realised other families didn't get given their own individual holiday itineraries and checklists two weeks before they went on holiday, and most families didn't stock check their cupboards monthly. How can he not remember to take his pills?'

'Things changed after Mama left.' Anna blew a frustrated breath. 'You were still at home then, Rosa. I know how self-centred you are, but surely even you noticed?' But then again maybe she hadn't; after all, hadn't Anna stepped in to run the household, juggling A-levels with housework and trying—trying and failing—to motivate her sister.

'I know you got bossier and more self-righteous than ever. I know you refused to move into halls during term time, staying at home to prove what a good daughter you were. At least until you started seeing that guy, then suddenly we saw another side of Anna…until he dumped you, that is. Then you got even more boring than before.'

Anna's chest tightened at the smirk on her sister's face. Would things be different if she had confided in Rosa then? Confided in anyone?

When had she decided it was safer keeping the rest of the human race at arm's length, caring more about the lives of people long dead than those who walked next to her? Until the last couple of weeks, that was. Somehow she had found herself allowing Leo further in than anyone ever before. At least he was upfront with her. He always walked away. He didn't want marriage, children, any emotional ties. That was fine with her. She wasn't equipped for any of that either. How could she be when she had barely lived?

'It's always lovely catching up with you, Rosa, but I have a lot to do. Good luck with those spreadsheets.' Anna turned, refusing to let the memories Rosa had stirred taint the sweet island air, the short time she had left with Leo. It would be nice if she and Rosa could spend ten minutes together without reverting to the squabbling children they had once been. It would be nice to have a sister, not an adversary.

'I'm just worried about you, Anna.' Rosa's voice stopped her in her tracks. 'Leo di Marquez isn't the kind of man you're used to...'

'I'm more than capable of handling Leo, thank you,' but even as she said it, Anna knew she wasn't being completely honest. Not with her sister and certainly not with herself.

'I just don't want a repeat of the Sebastian situation. I mean, he was an utter idiot, and Leo doesn't appear to be quite so arrogant, or as sleazy, but he broke you, Anna. I don't want that to happen again.'

Anna swallowed as the tears rose up, hot and ready. She had sworn never to cry over Sebastian again, but it was harder not to cry for the girl she had been, the naïve little idiot who believed in love and happy ever afters. 'Sebastian didn't break me, Rosa. I did that all by myself.'

It all looked so beautiful it almost hurt Anna to walk across the island, knowing all this was just temporary, that her life would soon revert to libraries and lecture halls. Over the last few weeks Anna had been probably the happiest she had ever been and that happiness wasn't just because of Leo. It was because the island felt like home. She loved putting it back together, planning for the future, knowing that everything she did made a difference. The thought of leaving physically hurt her.

But, if the island was home, then what was Oxford? Her old goals made no sense any more; she didn't care about being a youthful success or how many papers she could author. She wanted something real. Leo was right: she needed to find her story, not try and create one.

Not much of Valentina's lavish deposit was left, but the advance publicity had done wonders for bookings and it looked as if this would be the best summer for several years. Anna just hoped Sancia would be able to cope. At some point she would need to broach the island's future with her mother, but not till after the wedding, not while she was still this Anna, the Anna who went sailing out into the sea every evening once work finished, the Anna who had actually swum nude the other evening, the Anna who fell asleep wrapped around a shirtless pirate.

'Hey...' Speaking of shirtless pirates.

'Hey, yourself,' Anna said, unable to stop the smile spreading over her face as she drank Leo in. His tan had intensified over the last few weeks, his muscles gleaming under his golden olive skin, his hair grown out so it flopped over his forehead, adding a boyishness to his good looks, a boyishness that in no way diminished his aura of danger. 'Forgot your shirt again?'

'I know you like me half naked.'

Anna's knees weakened at the gleam in his eyes. She did prefer him like this, sweaty from the sun and manual labour, so different from the polished, fashionable playboy the world knew. 'You do add a certain aesthetic appeal to the island.'

Leo's grin broadened. 'You look remarkably empty-armed. I thought you went searching for the Final Checklist Clipboard.' Anna could hear the capitals in his teasing tones. Maybe she had put a lot of emphasis on just how important the checklist was.

'The clipboard? Oh, yes. That. You know, I think we can just as easily do the last walk through in the morning.'

'Oh?' Leo arched an eyebrow. 'You've changed your tune. I thought it was imperative we did that this afternoon or the whole timetable would go up in flames. What did you have in mind for the rest of the afternoon instead?'

'We—ell. I was thinking we could be spontaneous…'

'Spontaneous?'

'You, me, the boat.'

'Oh, that kind of spontaneous, *mi cariño*. Much as I was looking forward to inspecting every single one of the fifty-two bungalows, maybe I could be persuaded.'

Stepping closer, Anna ran a hand down his arm, enjoying the play of muscles under her fingertips, how soft his skin was, hot under her touch. 'Not in public,' she said softly. 'Boat first, persuasion later.'

His eyes darkened, flickering lust heating her through. Anna loved how her words, how her touch could elicit this response, how powerful Leo made her feel. 'Is that a promise, Anna?'

'A definite promise—and you know I always keep my word.'

'In that case,' Leo said, taking her hand in his, 'let's go. Right now.'

Just a few more days… Anna intended to make the most of every single moment.

Leo knew that Valentina's arrival would change things, he just hadn't realised how much, nor that he would find himself wishing for those halcyon days when it was just Anna and himself most of the time. Even though the main body of guests were still to arrive the island felt alive, buzzing, and it was impossible now to wander around and not see a living soul. Instead the maids bustled around, keeping the bungalows and public areas pristine, the groundsmen worked full time taming the greenery and ensuring the pools and courts were safe and inviting, and Leo couldn't sit down without a smiling server offering him a drink and snack. It was all very impressive, but not a patch on the informal friendliness of the island out of season.

But his happiness wasn't the point and his sister was delighted with everything. For a self-made millionairess who was marrying into old money Valentina had relatively simple tastes, and the lush green island ringed with beaches, the charming, white bungalows and the friendly staff captured her heart immediately. Especially when she had shyly outed herself to Sancia as Assumptia's daughter and been warmly embraced and welcomed home.

'Oh, Leo, it's perfect, even more perfect than I remembered. No wonder you couldn't tear yourself away. Or was it a certain hotel manager who kept you here?' she asked slyly. It hadn't taken her more than a few moments of watching Leo and Anna together to ascertain their situation, even though they had both been completely discreet, not a single lingering glance or touch in front of the guests.

'I just wanted to make sure everything was the way you want it,' Leo said, refusing to be drawn on his relationship with Anna, no matter how his sister teased him. 'How did I do?' He leaned back in his chair, smiling at his sister, her happiness so palpable she glowed.

Valentina had the biggest bungalow of all and Anna had worked hard to make sure it looked as bridal as possible, with sweet-smelling flowers in every room, and plenty of space for the bridal party to gather. Despite her intention to have a traditional Spanish wedding, Valentina had agreed to her husband's requests for a few American touches such as including bridesmaids and groomsmen and reception speeches. In return Todd had agreed to be escorted down the aisle by his mother and to an early evening ceremony, which would be followed by a party lasting well into the next morning.

'I can't wait for Todd to get here,' Valentina said for the twentieth time that day as she wandered around the elegant sitting room. 'This is beautiful, but it's far too big for one person.'

'Your mother would be really proud of you,' Leo said, guessing that his younger sister was thinking of her mother. At times like this Assumptia was never far from either of their thoughts. It was only four years since she had died; sometimes it felt like yesterday.

Valentina smiled. She didn't look like a media queen tonight, her thick mane of hair pulled back and her heart-shaped face free of any make-up. 'I hope so. She would love Todd, wouldn't she?'

'If you love Todd, she would love Todd,' Leo reassured her.

'I just want to be married. To be a wife and have a husband. To be part of a real family at last. Not that you're not an amazing brother, Leo, but I want to belong to someone, for someone to belong to me.'

Leo stared down at his bottle of beer. Valentina and he had almost instinctively decided to keep their relationship secret. She had wanted no connection to the father who rejected her, and Leo hadn't wanted the world knowing about the one good thing in his life. Valentina's knack for spin and brand management had ensured that any childhood stories she told began after Leo had introduced stability into their lives—tales of surfing and beach volleyball, fashion and fun. Her father, she claimed, had died before she was born. Her request for Leo to be part of her wedding would invite speculation, interest he had shied away from. But Anna was right. He needed to find his own way to be happy.

'Val, I want to walk you down the aisle. If you still want me to.' He wanted to be at her side on such an important occasion. Valentina's capacity for love, for forgiveness, for optimism, were the things he loved most about her. The things he envied most about her. His little sister was far braver than he was.

Valentina looked up, her eyes sparkling with tears. 'Leo? Really? Oh, thank you. It's the only wish I had left unfulfilled.' She leaned across and into him, as fragile as a bird, her bones clearly visible at her throat, the delicate blades at her back. She'd barely touched any food all day, Leo remembered, turned down wine for water; she hadn't even been tempted by the home-made lemon sorbet the cook had asked them to sample.

'I hope you start eating after this wedding,' he scolded her.

'Me too.' She squeezed his hand. 'It's just I have no appetite at all at the moment. Leo, don't tell anyone, it's too early, but I'm pregnant. You're going to be an uncle!'

CHAPTER TWELVE

'Pregnant?' Anna had curled up on the sundeck like a lazy kitten, basking in the sun, and at Leo's news she turned onto her back and stretched out. 'Is she happy?' For the first time in a long time Anna could hear the word without a pang of regret. Maybe she was finally moving forward.

'Ecstatic. Of course, this explains why she wouldn't postpone the wedding after the fire. For all her attitude and fashion sense there's a strong sense of traditionalist in Valentina. She will want to be married when the baby is born, for it to have the father she was denied.'

'Does she feel up to a big wedding if she isn't eating?'

'She says so. She says that she was dizzy for a couple of weeks, that she has been really nauseous and doesn't want to eat much, but she feels fine. She's really looking forward to the wedding, even if she will be toasting her husband with fruit juice.'

'And you'll be an uncle,' Anna teased. 'How do you feel about that? Don't worry,' she said as his face clouded. 'Every child needs an irresponsible uncle who buys them too much ice cream and lets them stay up far too late. I'm sure you will fill that role perfectly.'

'Is that my fate?'

'Afraid so.'

Anna looked up at the darkening sky, that same melancholy that had been chasing her all week shivering through her. Lucky Valentina, she thought. Marriage to a guy she adored, a baby on the way. She didn't seem to be worrying about her future, to be caught in a place she wasn't sure she wanted to be. Anna had been expecting a self-obsessed starlet demanding perfection from every tiny detail, creating drama for drama's sake, instead she had found Leo's sister to be a warm, intelligent young woman far more focussed on the marriage she was entering into than the wedding itself.

Pregnant. Anna's hand drifted down to cover

her own belly, memories of the brief weeks she too had carried life within her floating back. She had thought she was in love, yes, but she hadn't been secure. She'd been torn apart with fear over her future, how she'd manage work and a baby, worried about what Sebastian would say—and then once he knew she had had to deal with the crushing reality that she was on her own. That the man she thought she was in love with was just a fantasy, the reality someone completely and devastatingly different.

But within all that despair and pain there had also been excitement, a sense of wonder that somehow she was creating something real and tangible, not just words on a page. That she would have someone on her side, someone to really love, someone to love her unconditionally. Until that morning she had woken up writhing in pain and she'd known, long before the doctor had confirmed that the baby was no more.

She had never told anyone about her miscarriage until last week, until she found herself so unexpectedly confiding in Leo. Sebastian hadn't asked what happened, and she had spent the next two years avoiding anywhere she might see him.

Her father had been oblivious, Rosa too wrapped up in her own affairs, Sancia gone. No one noticed that Anna was slowly unravelling in a toxic mixture of guilt, self-loathing and heartbreak. Guilt thanks to that momentary glimmer of relief that the decision of whether or not to have the baby, to raise the baby, had been taken from her, that her life could continue on its foreordained path with no deviation. Self-loathing at her folly, at how easily she had been fooled, how easily she had fallen. Heartbreak that the man she loved didn't exist. She'd skipped lectures and tutorials for Sebastian, handed essays in late and badly researched. She still couldn't believe just how close she'd been to being 'sent down', expelled temporarily, or even expelled altogether. It had taken months to put herself back together, and to this day she knew that part of the girl she had been was still left back there in that damp Oxford winter.

It must be so different to be pregnant and to know that the baby was wanted by both parents, to celebrate every milestone, to have someone to sympathise with aching breasts, nausea, the extreme tiredness…

Hang on a second. Anna sat bolt upright, ice-cold fear flooding her. *She was a week late.* She was never late…

'Anna, have you got a minute?'

A minute? She didn't even have a second. She needed to get on a boat, get over to the mainland and drive to the nearest pharmacy straight away. 'Not now.'

Rosa took no notice. 'It's Jude. Valentina has asked him to the wedding and he wants me to be his plus one. Will that be a problem, I can still oversee the seating charts and things, and you'll be there with Leo anyway…'

What on earth was Rosa chattering on about? Anna pushed her hair out of her eyes. 'Leo hasn't mentioned me accompanying him to the wedding,' she said slowly. 'We're not, I mean, it's not serious.' Oh, God, Leo…no, she couldn't even think about Leo until she had taken the test and knew either way.

'Oh, come on, I've seen the way he looks at you.'

'It's not serious,' she repeated, Leo's words echoing through her. He didn't want anything permanent, had no interest in children. She would be on her own, just as she had been all those years ago.

'If you say so. So you don't mind? It turns out Jude knows Valentina quite well. He used to go out with one of the bridesmaids—the redhead who complained that the bed is too hard and that we haven't provided the right range of herbal teas—and it ended, well, horrifically. Long story short, she was involved with the book, so it's a pride thing to accept the invite and bring a date, I guess. But what with the way we left things, I think…'

Anna held up her hand to silence her sister and slowly counted to ten. 'Rosa, fill me in later. I have to go over to the mainland and I hate sailing over in the dark. Yes, go to the wedding. It's fine.' At any other point she would have wanted to know why Jude had asked Rosa to be his plus one, why Rosa was acting as if they were old friends, not new acquaintances, what book had sent Jude into such a spin and why Jude looked so damn familiar, but right now she didn't care. Let Valentina invite who she wanted to the wedding with just three days' notice. They'd deal.

'What's so urgent?' Rosa's voice sharpened. 'Are you okay? You're very pale. Do you feel ill?'

'Rosa, don't fuss. I just have to do something.'

'I really think you should wait till morning.' Then, as Anna shook her head, 'In that case I'm coming with you. I'll drive the boat. The way you look you won't be able to get it out of the harbour!'

Her first instinct was to refuse. She wasn't one for company at the best of times and now, with fear running through her veins, all she wanted was dark, brooding solitude. It wasn't as if she and Rosa were confidantes Anna knew more about some of her students' hopes and dreams than she did about her sister's. But somehow the decision was taken from her, Rosa not waiting for an answer, simply taking the boat key out of Anna's hand and leading the way down to the jetty. Leo's boat was clearly visible, the warning lights gleaming bright. At least he wasn't on there, having been bid to dinner with his sister and bridesmaids; at least Anna wouldn't have to pass him on her stealthy trip to the mainland.

Despite her desire for solitude Anna found herself surprisingly grateful for her sister's company. Rosa seemed to sense that she didn't want to talk and didn't press her for details, concentrating instead on steering the dinghy over the short distance as speedily as possible. She pulled up alongside the jetty on the mainland with a smooth flourish. 'Right, where next? Anna, I'm coming with you. Don't argue.'

Anna opened her mouth to protest and then shut it again. What was the point? Right now, someone else taking charge was blissful. Pulling the key to Sancia's ancient rusty small car from her pocket, she handed it to her sister, barely registering the moment Rosa's hand closed over hers with a reassuring squeeze. 'The town,' she said, her throat sore with suppressed tears. 'The pharmacy. There's one on the retail park this side of town. It's not far.'

The roads were deserted and it didn't take long to clear the small village and head towards the town. Rosa drove with the same careless confidence that characterised her every move, accelerating around every bend like a racing driver, her foot pressing the accelerator right to the floor so the car was almost vibrating as it sped along.

Normally Anna would tell Rosa to slow down, to insist she stop the car and let Anna take over, but this evening she was glad of the speed. The sooner she got her hands on that test, the better.

Think logically, she told herself. She was probably overreacting. Definitely overreacting. Just because she had only ever been late once before didn't mean there wasn't a perfectly reasonable explanation this time. Look at all the stress she had been under with her parents, Rosa, the wedding and her book. It made complete sense that her body would react in some way. It was only three weeks since she and Leo had sailed away to the mainland, three weeks since she had worn that little silk slip of a dress, three weeks since he had peeled it off her. It was far too soon for her to think she was pregnant. So what if, now she thought of it, her breasts were a little sore? So just the whiff of wine turned her stomach? There were one hundred explanations, none of which meant she was pregnant. And they had been careful, hadn't they? Of course they had.

They'd been careful, she reassured herself.

She had promised herself that she wouldn't

make the same mistake twice, but Anna knew all too well that not every promise could be kept.

Bright, neon lights broke the darkness. They'd arrived. Rosa swung the car into a free space and killed the engine. 'Do you want me to come in with you?'

'No. Thanks.' But now she was here Anna didn't think she could move.

'Anna, let me go.' Rosa had never sounded so gentle, so understanding. 'Do you need me to buy you a pregnancy test? Is that what's happening here?'

She was frozen, unable to form any words, to nod, to do anything but stare straight ahead and wonder how on earth she had managed to get herself into this situation again, how she could have been so stupid again. Did she have some kind of self-destruct button? A bat signal audible only to unsuitable men, instructing them to impregnate her then walk away, leaving her in pieces.

'Leo doesn't want a family.' That wasn't what she had intended to say. 'He'll think I've betrayed him.'

'Anna, honey, it takes two to make a baby.

Leo's a grown man. If you are pregnant, he'll understand.'

'No, he won't. He told me from the start, no promises, no commitment. It's bad enough I've fallen in love with him. How could I be so stupid as to get pregnant too? It's like Sebastian all over again, only much, much worse. I only *thought* I loved Sebastian.'

'You were pregnant back then? Why didn't you tell me? Why do you never let anyone help, Anna?' To Anna's surprise Rosa sounded like she was close to tears. 'You don't have to do it all alone. You don't have to be perfect. You can ask for help…'

'Last time I needed your help you walked away.'

Rosa bit her lip. 'Things were complicated then. I'm sorry. But I'm here now and I promise you, you're not alone. Now let me go and get the test for you and then, if you are pregnant, we'll figure out what to do. And if you're not then you and I need to have a long, overdue talk. Deal?'

'Deal.' Anna squeezed her sister's hand tightly then sat back and watched Rosa jog over to the store. When had her little sister got so wise?

So strong? At least it looked as if Anna wasn't alone. That was something. It had to be something. Right now it was all she had.

Leo had never been quite so grateful to leave his sister before. She'd been joined by her brides-maids, all intent on turning their first night on the island into an impromptu hen party. A beautifully choreographed, much photographed hen party, but one he had rapidly realised was no place for a red-blooded Spanish male. Especially not a red-blooded Spanish male who wanted to keep his dignity intact.

Wandering along the track that led to the villa, he realised he had no idea where to find Anna. Usually he found her almost by instinct, drawn to her wherever she was, but tonight her whereabouts eluded him. She'd been happy enough, lying on the sundeck on the boat, and then she'd gone strangely quiet before disappearing on some mysterious errand. He hadn't seen her since.

Her absence shouldn't bother him. After all, their idyll was nearly at an end. In three days' time Valentina would be married and his time on the island at an end. Time to sail on, to Nice or Monte Carlo, or maybe around the islands. Time to actually read some of the reports piling up in his inbox and move some money around. Time to resume his life.

The thought shouldn't feel so hollow.

But it did.

Leo exhaled, willing the negative feelings back into the box where he usually kept all emotions. What was the alternative? Anna would be returning to Oxford, burying herself back in her library, searching for the story to set her alight, the kernel she could turn into another book. That was where she belonged, Dr Anna Gray in her buttoned-up shirt. So different from his Anna, a sheet wound round her naked body, hair tumbling over her shoulders.

He always got bored with relationships first, that was what he'd told her—and he had been telling her the truth. He'd fully expected to be ready to leave her without a single pang of regret—which just showed what an idiot he really was. Right now all he felt was regret; their time together didn't seem finished.

But his biggest regret was knowing he would

do nothing to prolong the relationship. Knowing that he would just let her walk away and not lift a finger to stop her. Knowing he was too scared to try for something real, too scared to let her in, too scared to feel.

He deserved regret.

The courtyard was just ahead, lit by hundreds of small lamps, and as Leo turned towards it he glimpsed a silhouetted figure leaning on the archway, her slim build as familiar as his own reflection. She turned as he neared. 'Hey.'

'Hey yourself.' That leap of his heart, that lightening in his chest, they didn't mean anything other than his libido springing into life. *Keep telling yourself that, di Marquez.* 'You've been elusive this evening.'

'I had an errand to run.' Anna didn't return his smile, her eyes solemn in the lamplight. 'Leo, can we sit? I need to talk to you.'

'Sure, do you want a drink?'

'No, I'm not thirsty. Let's go find somewhere quieter, less busy.' She cast a quick look at the far table where her parents sat with Rosa and Jude, a board game set out on the table. Usually Leo would scoff at so cosy a scene, but tonight he was filled with a desire to walk over, pull up a chair and join in the teasing game, accuse Sancia of cheating with the rest of her family and challenge Professor Gray on every obscure academic word he insisted was within the rules.

It was a good thing their idyll was nearing its end. He was getting soft, weak, reverting to the needy boy he had once been.

Anna led the way through the trimmed-back greenery to the small beach at the furthest end of the island. There was no jetty here, no boats, no bar, the nearest bungalow a five-minute walk away. It had always been her favourite spot, she'd told him once, because it was quiet, facing out towards the sea, only the horizon in sight. It was so dark she had to use a torch to guide them there, but once they were on the beach the moon shone down and the tiny cove was illuminated by a thousand stars. Leo inhaled sharply, the beauty of the night cutting straight through the layers of cynicism, of irony, of humour with which he protected himself.

'There's no easy way of saying this.' Anna didn't make a move to sit down on the wooden loungers, invitingly laid out on the soft sand. Instead she stood on the very edge of the beach, her hands twisting together. The moon shone down, transforming her into a naiad of the night.

Foreboding stole into Leo, strong and knowing. Their idyll was over.

'Anna, what's wrong?'

She swallowed, but when she spoke her voice was clear. 'I'm pregnant. I'm sorry, Leo, but it's yours. I'm having your baby.'

CHAPTER THIRTEEN

FOR ONE SECOND, one tiny split second, Leo was aware of nothing but joy. Of hope, of redemption. But before he had a chance to register the feeling reality crashed back, cold and bitter.

What did he, Leo di Marquez, know about being a father? He, an unwanted son, an unworthy brother, untrustworthy lover? What did a man who couldn't commit to a home know about family? A man who knew nothing about love. Nonetheless, he knew his duty. 'Are you sure?'

The moment he spoke, the moment he saw Anna flinch—at his cold words, his cold tone—Leo knew the die was cast. In a way he was relieved; after all, it couldn't be any other way.

'I wouldn't tell you otherwise.' No, she wouldn't want to share fears or worries with him. They weren't a team after all. 'Turns out even I can't be careful enough. I don't know how it happened...' She swallowed, her eyes glistening in the moonlight before she snapped them shut, and when they opened her face was set. Determined. 'Don't worry, Leo. If you don't want to be involved you don't have to be. I'm quite capable of doing this alone. It's not the first time after all.' She looked so sad, standing alone in the moonlight, that Leo had to clench his fists to stop himself from heading over to comfort her. He had no right. He wanted no right. He could do this, but it had to be on his terms.

'I told you, Anna. I don't want a long-term relationship. I don't intend to have children. The family name dies with me.'

'You should have thought of that before. I didn't impregnate myself,' she snapped back and a small part of him applauded her courage, her fire. But he carried on as if she hadn't spoken.

'However, I know what has to be done, what has to be right. We will be married of course. You and the child will be under my protection.' He stood, straight and tall, and willed her to understand. This was all he had. All he was. But it was everything.

She didn't say anything for a long while and all Leo could do was stand and wait, trying to quell the myriad emotions jostling for prominence inside him, trying to shut them all down. Finally Anna sighed, a deep, bone-weary sigh, and wandered over to the nearest lounger, perching on it like a wary bird who knew it might need to escape at any time. 'I can't believe that this has happened again. That despite every precaution...' She paused, visibly fighting for control. When she spoke again, however, her voice was steady. 'I told myself all those years ago that I would never allow myself to be vulnerable again. That I would be focussed and strong. That I would never deviate from the plan, because I knew that way lay heartbreak. And then I met you...'

Silence fell and Leo welcomed it. Let every second excoriate him. He deserved it.

'I knew you were trouble. A poor little rich boy masquerading as a pirate, but I was so bloody sick of doing the right thing, I thought a few weeks out of the rigid life I allow myself wouldn't hurt, not if I was careful, not if I weighed up every risk and mitigated for it. I'm a fool.'

Every word fell straight onto his heart and left

its own scar. How could he contradict her? She had put her faith, her trust in him and he had nothing for her except a tarnished name.

'But, you know what, Leo? I'll be fine this time. I will do everything I can to nourish and carry this baby to term, and if I manage that, then I will love it and raise him or her to have compassion along with confidence. To dare to reach out for what they want, but not to trample others while they do it. And I'll teach them to love. Because that's the greatest gift I can give them. I'm sorry that you weren't given that gift. I'm sorry that you feel it's too late.'

She got to her feet and looked directly at him and Leo shivered at the sadness in her gaze, sadness for him, not because of him, and all the more devastating for that. 'Goodbye, Leo.'

She turned as if to leave. Had she not heard? 'Anna? You don't have to do this alone. I will marry you. I will be a father to your child.'

'Do you love me, Leo?' Her voice was so soft he could barely make out the words above the roar of the waves.

Love? He didn't even know what love was. But

he owed her too much to lie. 'Love isn't what's important here...'

She shook her head, dark tendrils caressing the nape of her neck. 'Love is all that matters, Leo. My parents couldn't make it, couldn't overcome all their differences even *with* love. How can we be a family without it? We'll fail before we start. I appreciate the offer, I really do. I know what it has cost you. But you're off the hook, Leo. I'm setting you free.'

And then she was gone and all he could do was stand alone in the moonlight and listen to the waves crash on the shore and wonder why, when Anna had made it so easy for him to walk away, he was rooted to the spot.

It was finally the night before the wedding. Earlier that day they had welcomed Todd, the groom, to the island, along with his family and groomsmen, and hosted a Spanish-style lunch for the entire wedding party. Four courses over several hours followed by much-needed siestas had made for the perfect introduction to the island, and Rosa had planned for beach games and a much more informal supper to be served at the beach later that evening. The informal evening would not only be fun, but crucially it gave the island staff plenty of time to prepare for the next day when another hundred guests were due to arrive and for the wedding ceremony itself, which would begin in the early evening.

Everything looked perfect. Every bungalow was ready, every tree had fairy lights threaded through it, the pagoda and central area were set up for the ceremony and party. Valentina's dress had arrived that day, escorted by a dressmaker who would stay until Valentina was dressed, and the chefs from Barcelona were already set up in the kitchen, working remarkably amicably with the island's own cooks. Valentina seemed delighted, her groom's wealthy parents approving and the bridesmaids—most of them—full of nothing but praise. If they could provide this level of service to the rest of the guests then the island's future would be secure. For now at least.

Four weeks of hard work coming to a climax. And all Anna could feel was limp relief. That was all she could allow herself to feel. Opening up the floodgates would come later, when she allowed herself the indulgence. For now all she could do was look at the unexpected turn her life was taking and do what she did best: plan. Notebooks filled with lists, budgets, ideas.

She hadn't seen Leo alone since two nights ago, keeping herself busy behind the scenes, but she knew he hadn't come to look for her once. He'd caught her eye today, at the lunch, when Anna had come out from the kitchen to check everything was okay. Her gaze had flown straight to him, despite herself; he'd sat with Todd's parents, but it was as if he had sensed her the second she stepped into the courtyard, his eyes instantly finding hers. Nausea hit her, swirling deep, as she did her best to calmly meet his gaze, trying to summon up a polite smile from somewhere. Trying not to read too much into his expression, trying not to tell herself that he looked haggard, as if he hadn't slept. Trying not to tell herself that he looked like a man facing into hell with no idea how he'd got there.

Anna knew she had to speak to him and tell him she understood. That she had met his parents. That she had held him while he slept, heard the muttered groans, enough words to know just how lost he truly was. That she knew he considered himself no more than the playboy he presented himself as, that he didn't believe he was worthy of love. That she loved him nonetheless, but had no intention of allowing him to destroy her life or their child's. But she couldn't bring herself to say the words yet. That she wasn't able to marry him, but he should be in their child's life regardless. That somehow they would make it work.

It was all so different this time round. She'd been so terrified before, unsure of herself, wanting someone to tell her that everything would be all right, desperate for Sebastian to be the man of her dreams, not the cold reality. She had no such illusions where Leo was concerned. He couldn't offer her what she needed and she loved him too much to accept less.

Raising a child alone wouldn't be easy, there were no guarantees, no certainties and all the lists in the world wouldn't change that, but she was strong. She could do this. She had to.

And she had to start by taking control of her life, of her happiness.

Anna took a deep breath and stepped into the

large sitting room. 'Mama, Dad, have you got a moment?'

'What is it, *querida*?' Yet again her parents were sitting together. For a couple who had separated a decade ago and barely spoken since they were awfully cosy. If Anna had one brain cell to spare on them she would be consumed with curiosity.

'I am going to make some changes, and I want to talk them over with you. Is now a good time?' She felt a little guilty. They had all been working flat out for days and this hour, while the guests took their siesta, would be the last peace they would know for the next week—but that was why she needed to talk to them now. She couldn't go into the next week without having some idea where she would be at the end of it.

'Of course,' her mother said. Professor Gray didn't say anything, but Anna hadn't really expected him to. He'd never been the curious type where his family were concerned. Sometimes she had been desperate for him to ask, just once, what was wrong.

'Okay, then.' She curled up on the padded window seat next to them. How many times had she sat here, in the tiled private sitting room, the family's only space on the entire island where they could just be themselves? It hadn't changed since she was a child, the same flower pictures on the walls, the same wicker side tables, the same comfy seats, the same stove in the corner for the brief but chilly winter. This was as much her home as the large house in Oxford—more so. The house belonged to her father's college and when he retired some other professor would move in, no matter that Anna and Rosa's initials were carved into the apple tree trunk in the garden, that Anna had recovered from her heartbreak in the attic bedroom.

'I need to make some changes in my life. I haven't been happy for a long, long time. I see that now. I thought work, success, might change that, but the harder I work, the higher I climb, the less I feel like me. It's as if the more lists I have, the more notes I take, the more control I think I have. But over the last few weeks I've realised I've been so busy chasing other people's stories I've forgotten to look for my own. And I think my story is here, at least, at the moment. Mama, I'd like to stay here, and help you run La

Isla Marina. How do you feel about that?' Anna held her breath as identical shocked expressions crossed her parents' faces.

Explanations could come later.

Professor Gray broke the silence first. 'What about your teaching? Your work? The offer from Harvard?' Anna looked keenly at her father. She hadn't realised he knew about the offer. Did he know she'd turned it down before—and why? 'You're doing so well, your book was so well-received, why throw it all away?'

'I stayed in academia, in Oxford, for you, not for me,' Anna admitted, the truth in her words bitter on her tongue. 'After Mama left you were so sad.' She shot a quick look at her mother, and flinched at the raw pain on Sancia's face. 'I just wanted to make you proud. Then I was so worried about you I couldn't bring myself to move out. I know, you're a grown man, you're the parent, Rosa and Mama told me that all the time. I think I just needed to be wanted, wanted to be needed. I like teaching, I like researching, but I'm only twenty-eight. The thought of doing nothing else for the next forty years fills me with fear, not anticipation. The truth is if I really wanted Harvard nothing would keep me away.'

'Is this just more of the same, *querida*?' Sancia asked, her dark eyes fastened on Anna's face. 'You think I need you to look after me now?'

'I did,' Anna admitted. 'Things were in a bad way here, and, I admit, I'm a little concerned that you're not coping.' She searched her mother's face in turn looking for clues. She should have asked what had happened earlier, not stormed in and taken over. 'But my original plan was to talk to you about selling, or bringing in a manager. I wouldn't even consider moving here if I didn't truly want to. I'll still write. Not the book I intended to. I'm thinking about writing about the island, the people who have lived here, how its fortunes have waxed and waned along with Spain's, a social history of Spain seen through La Isla Marina. We'll be independent, Mama, have our own tasks. Our own quarters. But only if you want me...'

Suddenly she was a child again, desperate to know she mattered, that she was wanted. Sancia's eyes softened. 'Of course I want you, *querida*. More than you could know.' Her voice broke on those words, and Anna's father took her hand. 'I haven't been much of a mother to you recently, have I? You just seemed so capable, Anna. You were always so much more in control than me. Things were difficult back then and I didn't feel like you needed me any more. That you could look after your father and Rosa so much better than I ever did.'

'I'll always need you, Mama.' Anna's voice broke as she felt the tears thick in her throat, burning her eyes. 'I needed you then, I need you now. Things were so hard and you weren't there.'

She'd never make the same mistakes, she vowed as her mother enfolded her in her arms, and for once Anna allowed her mother to bear her weight, to comfort her. She would always be there for her child, no matter what. Never let pride, or unhappiness or a misunderstanding drive them apart.

Sancia released her and wiped her eyes. 'I would love you to live here with me, to help me run La Isla Marina, *querida*, but only if you're sure this is what you want. Take your time, Anna. Go back to Oxford after the wedding and make sure you're doing what's right for you—and if so, we'll look at turning some of the unused rooms into an apartment for you.' Anna could tell her mother was teeming with unasked questions, about Leo, about what had really brought about this change in direction and she was glad her mother decided not to ask them just yet—although she knew Sancia wouldn't be able to keep silent for long.

In one way her decision had everything to do with Leo, and with the baby she was carrying. The baby she couldn't bring herself to mention to her parents, not just yet, not until after the wedding, until Leo had sailed away. But it went deeper than that. She liked the Anna she was here, even if she had messed up. She liked waking up to the smell of citrus and salt, she liked how every day was different, brought its own challenges and successes. She liked how her organisational skills were honed and used. She belonged here; she always had. It had just taken a couple of wrong turns to get here. And she couldn't imagine anywhere better to raise her baby.

'That sounds sensible.' Anna did her best to keep the surprise from her voice; she wasn't used to hearing sense from her mother. 'But the decision feels right. I won't change my mind.'

Getting to her feet, she leaned over to give both her parents a kiss, ignoring Rosa's quizzical look as she entered the room, a checklist in her hand. How long since they had all been together—and relatively amicably at that? The tension between Rosa and Anna had considerably lessened since the trip to the pharmacy. In fact Rosa had turned into somewhat of a confidante, never judging, always supportive. Maybe they'd never be best friends; they didn't need to be. They were sisters and they had a long-lasting bond no matter how different they were— and Rosa had promised to be an awesome aunt. Anna believed her.

'It all looks very cosy in here. Everything all right?' Rosa asked, looking directly at Anna. She knew of Anna's decision to wait until after the wedding to tell their parents about her pregnancy and was being, for Rosa, incredibly discreet. Probably because she seemed to be spending most of her time with Jude. Anna hadn't quite got to the bottom of what was going on there. All she knew was that they had dated a few years ago and for one reason or another it had fizzled out. They didn't look particularly fizzled right now—in fact the air practically sizzled whenever they were in the same space.

'Everything's good,' Anna said. 'I was just discussing the possibility of staying on the island. After all, it's never been one person's job to run it before.'

Rosa's eyes widened, a hundred questions clearly jostling for attention while she tried—and failed—to choose one. 'But... Oxford... Book... Dad... Here?'

'Quite,' Anna said enigmatically. 'Did you put the volleyball net up, Rosa? Don't worry, I'll go. I could do with some fresh air.' And she slipped out of the room aware her whole family were staring after her. She'd taken the first step towards deciding her future. All she had to do was let Leo know what she had decided. She couldn't avoid him for ever and she had to tell him how she felt. She knew it wouldn't change anything, she knew he had offered her all that he had, but she owed the truth to her baby—and she owed it to herself.

CHAPTER FOURTEEN

THE MID-AFTERNOON SUN was fierce, and Anna envied the guests, all sleeping off their lunch in the cool air-conditioned bungalows. 'Hats,' she muttered. She needed sun hats, a much bigger summer wardrobe if she really was planning to live here. Far fewer sensible pairs of trousers, more shorts. Vest tops and trainers instead of blouses and heels. The more she thought about it, the more sense her decision made on every level. Not least because she was itching to get started on her new book, to excavate all the island's secrets. She hadn't felt this fizz about her work since Joanna had been published. She'd missed it.

The beach games were to be played on the wide sea-facing beach on the far side of the island. Cricket, volleyball, boules and beach croquet had all been set up; the rules of at least three of the activities would be a mystery to most of the mainly Spanish and American guests. Anna walked briskly along the path with a new sense of ownership, of purpose. Every hour she put in here was an investment in her future, in her child's future. Hopefully. Her hands curled into fists; she knew all too well not to take anything for granted.

What was surprising her was how optimistic she was about the future. About the choices she was making. Of course she wanted things to be different, wanted Leo involved—*wanted Leo*—but she was strong. She had a family who weren't perfect, but who she now knew would support her, each in their own way.

'Hola.'

Anna jumped. She'd been so wrapped in her thoughts she hadn't even sensed Leo, let alone seen him. 'Hi.'

He fell into step beside her and they walked in silence. Funny, even when she had been actively hostile she had had things to say to him, any silences comfortable. Now, when there was so much to discuss, she didn't know where to begin. 'Todd seems nice.' Great, start with inanities.

'He is. He'll look after Valentina. Anna…'

Anna's heart stuttered as he said her name, that slow, languorous drawing out of syllables she loved. Her name, so prosaic, so boring, always sounded exotic when he said it.

'We need to discuss our situation. Marrying me may not be what either of us want, but it's the sensible thing to do. The right thing.'

'Leo…' How she wanted to tell him yes. To marry him, and hope that time would thaw him, that her love would be enough for the both of them. But she was too old and too wise to believe that was true. She couldn't do it to any of them; she had to be strong for all their sakes. 'I can't.'

He nodded, curtly, as if he had expected nothing less. 'In that case then I wanted to tell you that I will be leaving tomorrow. After the wedding.'

'Tomorrow? But the wedding is so late…'

'After the dinner, and the speeches. Before midnight.'

'Like Cinderella,' and she cringed at the startled look he gave her. 'I'm staying,' she blurted out, her throat swelling with the realisation that this really was it. He was leaving. Just as he had always said he would. She wasn't enough for him. The truth was nobody was. 'On the island. I'm going to help Mama run everything and write from here. Look for the story, not the most impressive display of research.'

'You'll need a new notebook.' Leo's smile didn't go anywhere near his eyes.

'Several.'

'Here.' He handed her a card. Anna turned it over, trying to make sense of the type. An email address—not his—a number. 'This is the best way to contact me, through my business manager. If you need anything, get in touch. I'll arrange for a monthly allowance...'

'I don't need your money.' The words came out more harshly than she intended and as he flinched she felt a moment of victory. 'Please. You can still be involved, even if we're not married.'

'I don't know how, Anna. I need some time.'

Anna stopped and turned to him, raising her hand to cup his cheek one last time, closing her eyes as she felt the rasp of his skin against hers, breathed in the scent of him. 'You do know how, if you'd just let yourself feel. You're so much more than you allow yourself to be, Leo. I think you've been playing a part so long you've forgotten who you really are. The sad truth is, the only person you have ended up hurting is yourself, even if you don't see it.'

She dropped her hand, instantly aching to touch him again. 'The sad truth is…' she repeated, taking a deep breath, knowing she would regret not saying the next words, even if they scared her. 'I like who I am with you. Like who you are with me. I think we're good together. You challenged me, made me step back from my path and take a look around, re-evaluate who I was and what I wanted. And I think you were real with me, you were honest. Which is why you're running. Because that scares you. Honestly? It scares me too. I didn't expect this, didn't want it, but here we are.'

'You seem to be forgetting,' he drawled, 'that you are the one who turned me down. I offered to marry you, Anna. You said no.' The shutters were up now. He was the bland playboy of the photos, not the pirate who had captured her heart, not the confidant who made her think and challenge herself. Anger flared up; this was her life he was messing with now, her happiness he spurned.

'I don't need marriage, Leo. All I need is your heart. Because you have mine. I love you, Leo.' A flare of something she couldn't read in the dark eyes at her words—anger, passion? Before she could get a handle on the heat it faded and he was back to bland. She pressed on. 'I know that wasn't the deal, wasn't what you wanted, but I couldn't help it. I'm in love with you, Leo. Not with your father's title, or the playboy, or the money, or the looks. With the man who spent a month fixing up an island for his sister. With the man who refuses to play his family's games. With the man who puts integrity before an easy life. With the man who listens to me. With the man who makes me feel beautiful.'

'You are beautiful,' he said hoarsely.

Anna stood there, knowing her heart was in her eyes, on her face, knowing she had nothing else to say, to give, hoping it was enough. And for one moment she thought it might be, her heart speeding up as Leo took her hand in his, only to drop it and step away. 'I'm sorry,' he said and then he was gone, leaving her alone on the path.

'There you are, *mi hermano.*' Leo hadn't even realised that he had ended up at Valentina's door until she stood before him, worry etched on her picture-perfect face. 'Do you know I have barely seen you over the last three days? I was hoping we could spend some time before the wedding together.'

'I'm sorry.' Lately he seemed to spend a lot of time apologising to women he had let down. 'I've been busy.' Looking at his sister, he frowned. She was dressed in a bright orange bikini top and white shorts, her hair twisted up in a complicated braid. He recalled the extensive itinerary which Anna—his heart stuttered, of course it was Anna—had ensured each guest had copies of. 'You're off to the beach games? It's a bad time. I'll let you get on…'

'No, Leo.' Valentina caught his hand. 'I'm not playing. I know it's silly superstition, but I don't want Todd to see me before the wedding…'

'You might have thought about that before choosing to get married on a small island where you're never less than fifteen minutes from each other.'

'True, which is why I've arranged for Todd to spend tomorrow on a boat trip. By the time he gets back I'll be getting ready in here, so we'll be quite safe. It's just tonight, and I don't mind missing the games, especially if it means we get the chance to catch up. You've not been yourself, Leo.'

Of course she'd noticed. She was wasted on modelling. His little sister would make a great detective.

'I'm fine.'

'Hmm?' Valentina raised her eyebrows at him. 'Come in, sit down. There's some bottled water, want some?' She waited until he was safely sitting on the sofa, a cold drink by his side, before pouncing. 'You've been avoiding the pretty manageress.'

'Anna? I'm not avoiding her. It's just complicated.'

'How? You like this girl, Leo! I've seen you

with her. You're like a different man. No masks, no pretending…'

Each word hit home. He had been a different man this last month. A happier man. But happiness didn't last. 'She's pregnant, Val.'

His sister stilled. 'What?' and to Leo's horror her eyes filled, one large tear rolling—in the most photogenic way—down her face. 'Leo,' she breathed, reaching for his hands and clutching them. 'That is wonderful. Our children will be cousins, will be friends. They will grow up with family around them, not like us, huh? Better than us.'

'It's very early, Val, don't tell anyone.'

'No, no, of course. Oh, but, Leo. This is what I have prayed for. I am so happy and now you have happiness too.'

The only way Leo managed to get through every long second was by staying numb. It was something he had a lot of practice in, he'd learned long ago to school his face, his very thoughts, but Valentina's sheer delight in his news tore through his defences. 'We're not together, Anna and I.' The words were wrenched from him.

'You're having a child together. What else do you need?' The certainty in Valentina's voice would almost be comical in any other situation. There was the grit that had helped her rise to the top of her profession.

'Val, I asked her to marry me and she said no.' Saying the words allowed hurt in in a way he had never imagined possible. But then Anna had just poured her heart out to him. Had given him her heart and he had done nothing. He deserved the pain.

'She turned you down? Why?'

'I'm not enough. Not to be a father, or a long-term father. Anna deserves better, she deserves more. I don't know how to love her. To love anyone.' To his shame his voice cracked as he said the words. She did deserve more, but how he wished he were the man to provide it.

Taking his hand in hers, Valentina sat next to him, leaning in, giving him her warmth and support. Leo had always been the big brother, the one who took care of her, proud to hand over his pay checks to help with rent; when had his little sister got old enough to start taking care of him? 'Mama always said you were the saddest child she'd ever known. She said leaving you broke her heart. She'd never known a child who stood so stiffly when she cuddled him before. She was so happy when you came back into her life. Our lives.

'Leo, you gave up university and got a job to help pay our rent. I know you spent that first year working on a building site until your investments paid off because of us. You looked after me when I was a child. You were the one who held me when Mama died. You were the person I needed to give Todd his seal of approval. You are the person I want by my side tomorrow. My child is so lucky to have you as an uncle, and that baby Anna is carrying is lucky to have you as a dad—and me as an aunt,' she added with a cheeky grin. 'The only person who doesn't believe in you is you. How does she make you feel? In here?' She tapped his chest, right over his heart.

'She makes me feel…' Anna's words came back to him with devastating clarity. *All I need is your heart. Because you have mine.* Was that what they had been doing? Exchanging hearts during those long, hot nights? Those intense conversations? That baring of souls?

Leo closed his eyes and all he could see was Anna. Anna standing there with that notebook in her hands, blue eyes blazing as she ordered him off the island. Anna dirty and hot, paint all over her shorts, determined to make sure every single inch of the bungalow she painted was perfect. Anna glowing as she told him once again how misunderstood Joanna the Mad was. Anna icier than he imagined possible confronting his parents. Anna, hair tumbling over her shoulders, wrapped in a sheet. Anna supine on the sundeck of his boat in nothing but a tiny bikini and an inviting smile.

He liked every single Anna, wanted every single Anna. Wanted to possess her, protect her, make her laugh, tease her, provoke her, seduce her. Was that love? How did a person know?

'Leo? Do you love her?'

'How can you bear it, Valentina? Putting your trust in one person? Your heart?' The words were torn from him.

'How can I bear not to?' she said simply. 'Leo, I would much, much rather give it my all and let it all go horribly wrong than never try. There's no guarantees. I was luckier than you, I know that. We had no money, but I always knew I was wanted, knew I was loved. And if I lose all this…' her expansive gesture took in all the trappings of success littering the sitting area: the deceptively simple cashmere cardigan, the flip-flops and beach bag that cost more than a second-hand car, the luxury hand lotion on the table, the huge diamond glittering on her hand '…I can cope. I know how to work. But I can't live without love. I don't want to. So tomorrow I put my faith, my trust in Todd. I wish you could have the same faith, *mi hermano*.'

Leo stayed with Valentina for the rest of the evening. She'd arranged for a simple salad to be delivered to her bungalow, and the two ate, sharing stories of Assumptia as they did so. 'I wish she had met Todd,' Valentina said wistfully. 'Wish she was here to celebrate tomorrow, wish she could meet the baby. But I know she would be so happy you are here by my side, Leo. And I know she would want you to take a leap of faith. To believe in love, to believe you are worthy of love. Because you are, more than you know.'

Leo kissed his sister goodnight, promising to be back in the morning, and set off down the lantern-lit path towards the dock and his boat. He had sailed it to the mainland for cleaning and restocking just a few days before, but if he was setting off with no known destination tomorrow then he needed to give it a quick check-over. But as he reached the dock he found himself rooted to the jetty, unable to climb into the small dinghy. This would be the last time he would sail over to his boat knowing he would be returning to the island, to Anna. Tomorrow he wouldn't simply fasten the dinghy to the boat, but would stow it and when he pressed the throttle it would be to sail away for ever.

Staring out at the moon-kissed waves, Leo didn't feel the usual sense of freedom, of adventure. Did he really think his absence was better for Anna and for the baby? That a loveless marriage of convenience was the only other answer? Or was he just too afraid to put his heart on the line? He who was so contemptuous of his father's fear of public dishonour was just as afraid himself. Not of being publicly humiliated, but of being found wanting. Far easier to steer clear of intimacy than risk rejection.

Truth was, he hadn't intended to leave quite so soon, hadn't intended to break things off with Anna. Not yet. Not until fear had precipitated his decision. If there were no baby then he would be looking forward to tomorrow, to dancing with her, steering her into a secluded corner, sweeping her away from the festivities and back to the boat. Thoughts of her consumed him—would those thoughts disappear with the miles or would she continue to haunt him?

And there was a baby. Right now just a vulnerable bunch of cells, but a bunch of cells that would divide and grow into a child. Would it have Anna's blue eyes or his own brown ones? What would it think of him? Would it resent him for not being there? Despise him for being a coward? Ironic, he'd spent his childhood desperate for his father's love and approval. Valentina had just wanted a father to acknowledge her. Did Leo really think that throwing money Anna's way would make him a better man? He of all people should know that money solved nothing.

He'd told Anna that she was the bravest person he knew. Anna who used her notebooks and lists as a shield. Anna who had been hurt by her family, but who had the courage to love them regardless, to keep trying, keep loving. Anna who had been so scarred by her last pregnancy yet who faced this new one with resilience and with hope. Anna who loved him, who believed in him, who wanted nothing from him except what she was prepared to give in exchange. Anna who was stronger than he could ever be.

Did he love Anna? And if so did he have the courage to be vulnerable before her, with her? All Leo knew was that he couldn't carry on this way. Couldn't be this lonely and survive. Something had to give before he broke and the only person he wanted, the only person he needed was right here on La Isla Marina. If he was brave enough to find her. Brave enough to let her in. Brave enough to love.

CHAPTER FIFTEEN

IT WAS A perfect evening, as if Valentina had ordered the weather along with the tiny cakes, the *piñatas* hanging from the tree, the tasteful wedding favours. Not a cloud marred the pristine blue sky, the late spring sun warm rather than scorching. The day had been manic with last-minute wedding preparations, checking in the hundred-plus guests who'd arrived that day, and taking care of the myriad tiny problems that popped up, from a blocked shower to a loose tile, the wrong brand of herbal infusions to forgotten toiletries. It was all going to be worth it though. Most of the guests, on Valentina's side anyway, were young, beautiful and had thousands of social-media followers. The island had been photographed hundreds of times—the trees, the fairy lights, the boats, the beach, the bathrooms. No detail was apparently too small for a filter and a fitting hashtag: *#valwedding #spanishheaven* and the ubiquitous *#blessed*. They wouldn't have been able to buy that kind of publicity with an unlimited budget and a crack PR team.

The best thing about being so busy was that Anna didn't have time to think about Leo or his imminent departure. To feel upset or humiliated that Rosa was attending the wedding with Jude while she stayed firmly in the background as staff, dressed in the same black skirt and white blouse as the rest of the female staff, hair tied back, a world apart from the glamour of the guests.

She just had to get through today and then Rosa would take over for the week of post-wedding festivities, all already planned and organised, the departure of the wedding guests next week and the resumption of normal holiday guests. Usually they would have a couple of months at half capacity before the summer madness, but thanks to the Valentina effect they were fully booked right through to October and Anna had a list of brides wanting exclusive use of the island next year.

Next year… Her hand crept to her stomach. Things would be very different next year.

She crossed her fingers. *Please let this one be healthy.* Anna had never quite forgiven herself for that momentary sense of relief ten years ago when she realised nothing need change, that she could go back to university and resume her life. The guilt contributing to the depression that had dogged the rest of her first year and still flared up if she wasn't careful to heed the warning signs. Guilt and grief a toxic mixture.

Sometimes she wondered how her life would have turned out if she hadn't miscarried. Would she have the career she had now or would ambition have been sacrificed to the demands of single motherhood? Either way there would be a nine-year-old running around now. When Anna closed her eyes she could picture her—it was always her—a skinny dark-haired child with Sebastian's green eyes. She'd never forget her ghost baby, never not love her, never not want forgiveness.

Which was why she had to concentrate on this baby. Not allow Leo's departure to send her spiralling, to stay strong and healthy and to count her blessings every single day. Be grateful Leo had been in her life even for so short a time, had helped her see a new way.

The sound of the traditional Spanish band starting up a lively tune pulled Anna back to the here and now and she straightened, pulling at her skirt to neaten it. She had elected to stand with the rest of the staff at the back of the tree-lined clearing where the wedding and party were being held. The official stood waiting, due solemnity on her face, and the guests were sitting in lines facing the pagoda, an aisle separating the two sides, wide enough for the bridal party to proceed along.

Valentina had kept the bridal party outfits simple with cream linen suits for the grooms-men and red knee-length dresses for the brides-maids, the full skirts and hint of ruffle a nod to Valentina's Spanish roots. The six couples proceeded along the aisle, lining up along the front, either side of the pagoda, ready to welcome the bride and groom. First Todd, his mother on his arm, solemn faced and nervous. Anna loved the Spanish custom of letting the groom's mother walk him down the aisle, a lump forming in her throat when Todd kissed his mother's cheek as he handed her into her seat, then turned to watch his bride proceed down the aisle.

Valentina looked glorious. The bodice clung like a second skin, accentuating her tiny waist and curves before flaring out into a full knee-length skirt. She'd opted for white rather than the traditional Spanish black, with a sheer overdress embroidered with bold, beautiful red flowers, her hair loose and unfettered except for the matching flower in her hair. Anna's eyes skimmed over the breathtaking bride, all her attention on the man accompanying her down the aisle. Leo, devastating in a cream linen suit. Anna drank him in, imprinting every detail on her memory. How the dark hair fell over his forehead, the broad shoulders, the unconscious grace with which he carried himself. She blinked back hot tears. Four weeks of memories weren't enough. Not nearly. But they were all she had.

Leo looked preoccupied, all his attention on the ceremony, the vows, the readings. Anna knew that Todd and Valentina had actually married quietly in New York earlier in the week to cut down on the paperwork, but considered today their real wedding day, Valentina openly crying as she made her vows and the couple presented each other with *arras*, coins that represented their commitment to each other, and the wedding rings, which Valentina wore on her right hand, as was usual in Spain, and Todd on his left.

And then it was done. They were married. Time to swing into action, make sure the drinks and canapés were circulated, put out the tables and chairs while the photos took place, and check on the kitchens and the performers who had been booked to entertain the guests. Anna stepped back into the trees. Leo still hadn't looked at her. Not once.

The ceremony was over, the food had been eaten, drinks drunk, bands had played, speeches made, the *detalles* handed out and the bride and groom had taken to the floor to perform a very sexy and perfectly choreographed tango. Now Jude had taken centre stage and, accompanied only by his guitar, was serenading the happy couple with a ballad Leo vaguely recognised. Couples swayed to and fro under the lantern-lit scene, Valentina and Todd right in the centre, eyes locked as they danced. Leo swallowed. This was when he had been planning to slip away, all his duties done.

He looked around, but there was no sign of Anna. He had caught glimpses of her during the evening, like a ghost at the wedding, unobtrusive in her staff uniform, her hair pulled severely back. Every time he had gone to intercept her she had slipped away. He couldn't tell if she was purposefully avoiding him; he did know that she hadn't once caught his eye.

Rosa was sitting near the pagoda, her gaze fixed on Jude. Leo swallowed his annoyance. Anna's sister hadn't been carrying drinks or trays of food; she hadn't sponged marks off dresses or attended to torn hems or got more ice because the water wasn't chilled enough. No uniform for her, instead a lemon-coloured dress that set off her tan, her hair intricately braided as it fell down her back. Leo pulled a chair up next to her. 'Where's Anna?'

The hostility in Rosa's eyes was a shock. Was this a forewarning of the reception he could expect from Anna? 'I thought you were leaving.'

'I need to speak to Anna.'

'Maybe she doesn't want to speak to you.'

'Maybe,' Leo acknowledged. 'It's important, Rosa, please.'

Rosa sat staring at the stage, her face set. 'She'll be back at the villa. She's overseeing the clean-up and packing.'

'Packing?'

'She's heading back to Oxford tomorrow.'

'I thought she was staying here?'

'Mama wants her to go back and think about it. It's a huge change. Everyone just wants her to be sure. To make sure she's doing it for the right reasons.' The glance she slanted at him was unreadable.

'Thanks.' He got to his feet.

'Leo? She's actually doing really well. If you are going to make matters worse then stay away or I'll make you sorry you ever messed with my sister.' And she turned her attention back to the stage, clearly dismissing him. Leo stood for a second, staring at her slim, determined form.

'Warning understood,' he said and walked away.

The whole island thrummed with activity, the music permeating every corner, lights illuminating every path and cove. There were no hidden corners; people seemed to be everywhere in groups or couples, dancing, talking, embracing. It wasn't midnight yet; the party would go on for hours, probably until dawn. A couple of times people tried to intercept him, to draw him into the festivities, but Leo's attention was focussed on the ornate villa at the centre of the island and the woman within it.

The reception area was quiet, although he could hear a hubbub from the kitchen, and Leo looked around before slipping through the door that he knew led to the personal family rooms. It looked as if an entire wing of the villa was for family use. The wide hallway he stood in led to a huge sitting room, a study and a small kitchen, stairs winding up from the far end. Leo headed for the stairs and the next floor. Bedrooms, bathrooms, all unoccupied, and another staircase, winding up to the turret. Of course Anna's bedroom would be up here. A princess in a tower dreaming of kings and queens and adventure. The door was open and he stepped in.

The small, octagonal room was a contrast to the luxury of the bungalows. A simple rug on the tiled floor, an iron bedstead covered in bright blankets, a trunk filled with clothes. But there were windows on three sides looking out over the island and a certain quirky charm to the room, which suited Anna. She'd been sitting on the bed when he stepped in and she stood up slowly, the colour draining from her face.

'Leo, what are you doing here? I thought we'd said all there was to say.'

'Rosa told me where you were. You're leaving?'

'You don't have the monopoly on running away.'

'Is that what you're doing?'

'Yes, no—I need time to think. To sort my affairs out. To sort myself out. I *am* coming back though. I've made my mind up. This is where I belong.'

Leo looked at her. At the dark shadows under her blue eyes. She'd lost weight over the last few days, her cheekbones a little more prominent. Anger rose in him, hot and thick. He was responsible for all of it.

'What does Sancia think about you staying?'

'Thanks to Valentina we're booked up well into next year. I'm not sure there will even be an off season this year. If we can heat the bungalows properly we might be able to open all year round. Mama is relieved, I think. Surprised, but relieved. We've come to a new understanding. I think there is more to be said, but we're in a good place. I think we'll work well together.' Leo recognised the matter-of-fact tone, the way Anna looked at the list lying on the bed. She was protecting herself with facts. Protecting herself from him.

Regret burned deep, regret and apprehension—and hope. 'How would she feel about a full-time painter and decorator living on the island too?' His heart hammered as he said the words, his pulse beating louder than the drums on the stage outside.

Anna just stared. 'We have the groundsman. I guess if we need another person we could hire them…'

'I mean me.'

Her eyes flew to his, hope mingling with wariness and a hint of anger. 'What do you mean *you*?'

'I mean I could stay on full time.'

'Is this the next stage in the *annoy your par-*

ents crusade? Full-time gambler to handyman? Because the only teen rebellion I'm interested in will be happening in around thirteen years' time.'

There was so much he needed to say. Wanted her to hear, but he didn't want to do it here surrounded by her suitcase and piles of clothes. Her lists and notebooks. He needed neutral ground. Leo held out a hand. 'Walk with me? Please?'

It hurt to see how long it took her to decide, to see the conflicting emotions pass clearly across her face before she finally nodded, although she made no move to take his hand. 'Ten minutes. I have a lot to do.'

Silently they left the room, heading back downstairs and slipping out of the side door back into the moonlit night. The sound of the band wafted clearly across the night air, along with the hubbub of over one hundred people enjoying themselves. Without speaking they turned away from the noise, heading to the far end of the island, to the cove where just three nights ago Anna had turned his world upside down— and he had broken her heart.

Leo searched for the right words to show her

he was serious, to tell her what was in his heart. He had no practice, no experience at this type of honesty, at laying himself bare—and the stakes had never been higher.

'My wish to stay here has nothing to do with my parents. Anna, I turned up here lost. So lost I could just sail across to La Isla Marina and know that no one, nowhere would miss me. So lost I could just stay for a month knowing no one would even notice. I came here with no agenda, no expectations and yet I was happier than I think I've ever been. Every day I achieved something, made something, did something. And then there was you.'

'Me?' Her voice a whisper.

It was now or never. All Leo knew was that he had to try. That he had to convince Anna, show her that he loved her. That even if she still didn't want to marry him he would be the best father possible for the baby. Their baby. That she had changed his life, changed him. He just needed to find the words. Tell her that he had always thought he was no one, nothing, but Anna made him realise he knew he was someone worth being. 'You. Infuriatingly organised, superior, sexy as hell you. You took one look at the façade I presented and dismissed me as being beneath your notice—and then you took a second look and I was defenceless.'

Anna didn't know what to say or where to look. She'd reconciled herself—well, she was doing her best to reconcile herself—with Leo's departure, with knowing that all foreseeable future contact would be via a business manager, that she couldn't save him after all. And now here he was, by her side, telling her everything she wanted to hear. But how real was he? Hope rose, treacherous and seductively sweet, no matter how she tried to clamp down on it. 'You want to stay here and what? Be the handyman?' she said, trying to make some sense out of the senseless and failing.

His mouth quirked into a smile. 'I want to be with you. I'm just trying to sell it to you in practical terms, because I know you'll want to make a pro and con list and so I thought I'd get straight in there with the practical reasons. I can run my business from here, but I can also help you run this place, help it grow, be the place you want it to be. The place your grandparents wanted it to be.'

'You are pretty handy with a paintbrush.' She couldn't believe she'd just said that, but she had no idea what else to say, what to think. Not quite believing this was happening despite the sincerity in Leo's eyes, in his voice.

'When I asked you to marry me I expected you to turn me down. Why would a woman like you marry me? You're not impressed by money, by titles and I thought I had nothing else to offer. I was too scared to look deeper.'

'I wanted to say yes,' Anna whispered. 'More than you'll ever know. But how could I marry you when you wouldn't let me in? Once I might have thought that was okay, despite my parents' break up, despite my own instincts. But I'd glimpsed more—and I couldn't settle for less. I can't settle for less. Not once I realised just how much I love you. It's not fair on me or you.'

'I'm sorry, Anna. I let you down. I reacted badly. I was so used to expecting nothing from my life and then there you were and I had this vision of a whole other life. Of a family and a place in the world. It was all I ever wanted once, but

I gave up on that hope many years ago. I don't know how to be a father. How to be a husband. But I've realised that's okay. I just need to try. To trust in you. In us.'

They had reached the cove and Anna sank thankfully onto a bench, trying to quell the trembling in her legs, her hands, to make sense of it all. She wanted to believe that Leo was here, was trying again because he had realised he was head over heels in love with her, but he hadn't spoken of love. He wanted to do the right thing by her—and that was laudable, of course it was, but how could she say yes when she loved him? When nothing had changed? She remained convinced of one thing: a one-sided marriage would never work.

She stared out at the dark vastness of the sea, the whisper of the waves calming her, giving her the strength to turn to him. 'Leo, listen to me, you don't have to marry me for the baby. We can raise it together. And it's still such early days. I know what can happen, how wrong things can go, how quickly it can all change. Don't make promises…don't change your life for what might be.'

'I know it's early, and I know you're scared that you might lose it, and I can't make you any promises except I will be here no matter what, and that I want to marry you no matter what. I love you, Dr Anna Gray. I made a list…'

The shaking in her hands intensified. Had he just said love or were her ears hearing what they wanted to hear? 'You made a *what*?'

'I didn't think you'd believe me otherwise. I know you're a great believer in a good list. I was talking to Valentina yesterday, about all the reasons you're too good for me, and I went home and wrote them down. And that's when I realised. They're not just the reasons why you're too good for me. They're also why I love you. And why I would be a fool to let you go. My life had no meaning, Anna, has no meaning without you. I need you and I love you and I want to marry you.'

She had no idea what to say, what to think, her mouth was dry, her blood thumping, hope tantalising her every breath. 'Do you have the list?' She needed proof, evidence, something tangible to believe in.

A smile curved his mouth, seductive and

wicked. 'It's back on the boat, but I know it by heart.' Leo knelt by her side, capturing her hands in his as he looked into her eyes, his own shining with sincerity, with hope. With something that looked a lot like love. 'I love how you pretend to be so sensible, but then you can be so spontaneous. I love the way you eat *gambas* with no inhibitions. I love the way you look after your parents even though they drive you mad. I love the way you talk about people who are long dead as if you met them yesterday. I love every notebook, every list. I love the way you spent every hour making sure Valentina had the perfect wedding. I love how patient you are with the most unreasonable guest. I love how dangerous you are when riled. I love the way your eyes get hazy just before I kiss you. I love your mouth and your eyes and your hair. I love your determination. I love you, Anna.' His voice broke and he was looking at her with an intensity, with a passion she had never seen before. An intensity that called to her, completed her. 'I don't deserve you, but I promise to learn to. Please, Anna, *mi corazón*, will you marry me? For the right reasons. Because I love you and you love me and I want us to be a family, together.'

'Leo.' The words wouldn't come; all she could do was hold onto his hand as if it were a lifeline and let the hot tears flow. Tears of relief, of happiness, of love. 'Are you sure?'

'I couldn't be surer. I've spent my whole life sailing from place to place, searching for something, someone to make me feel, to believe in myself, never believing I would find it. Too scared to put my faith in anyone, too scared to trust, terrified of always being alone, but never seeing another way. I knew as soon as I saw you, a sea nymph on the shore, that my life would never be the same again. I love you, Anna. You make me a better man. Let's build a life together here, raise our children here and continue your grandparents' legacy.'

Anna searched his face, looking for traces of the bland playboy, the practised mask, but all she could see was love. Love mingled with hope and resolve and finally she began to believe. Believe that Leo loved her as she loved him, believe that happiness might be in her grasp if she was brave enough to trust in him, believe that she could take a chance on the unknown. 'Yes,' she said, her grasp tightening on his. 'Yes, Leo. I will marry you.'

If she had any lingering doubts, the joy on Leo's face instantly dispelled them. *'Mi amor,'* he breathed, pulling her to her feet and enfolding her in his arms, and as his head bent to hers, in a kiss of infinite tenderness, of love, Anna knew it wasn't only Leo who had finally come home. She had as well, and right here, in his arms, was where she belonged.

* * * * *

LET'S TALK

Romance

For exclusive extracts, competitions
and special offers, find us online:

f facebook.com/millsandboon

⦿ @millsandboonuk

🐦 @millsandboon

Or get in touch on 0844 844 1351*

For all the latest titles coming soon,
visit millsandboon.co.uk/nextmonth

Want even more
ROMANCE?

Join our bookclub today!